Daycare Whispers

MariaLisa deMora

First Published 2026

ISBN 13: 978-1-971653-07-5

DEDICATION

Little Miss: "I want a 'jeawous sangwich."' (part of my job is deciphering 3-year-old speak). "A jealous sandwich?" I enquire. ...uh, a what? "Yes, wif a hot dog, and bwead, and pickle jeawous. A jeawous sangwich!" Pickle jealous? Oh...pickle relish. Gocha kid. Problem decoded, solved, and jealous sandwich delivered. ~ Kristen Merritt Gowan

For all the exhausted caregivers out there who still make time to laugh at the kidisms.

Contents

ACKNOWLEDGMENTS

Thank you, reader. Your support means more than you'll ever know.

This book flowed really easily, something I'll never take for granted again. The process of building a world can be so engrossing, it's a commitment that I love to make. Hope y'all enjoy it as much as I have!

Thank you to Becky and the gals at Hot Tree Editing, you make every word better and I appreciate you.

Thank you to my wonderful neighbors, who gathered around me when I was hurt and ill, and have stayed a tethering force in my world. Diana and Tina, I don't know what I would have done without your friendship. Y'all rock!

Woofully yours,
~ML

Daycare Whispers

In the whispering winds of Willow Creek, where misty valleys cradle storybook charm, Sunnybrook Cottage Daycare is a beacon of giggles, crayons, and innocent wonders. Until a child's faint murmurs unravel threads of long-buried secrets that refuse to stay silent.

Daycare Whispers is a heartwarming cozy mystery overflowing with small-town allure, hilarious kid quips like "Whispers tickle my ears like sneaky fairies!" and spine-tingling suspense that keeps the pages turning. *Wall Street Journal* and *USA Today* bestselling author MariaLisa deMora delivers the third installment in the Sunnybrook Cottage Cozy Mysteries series, where stakes whisper as softly as a child's secret yet cut as deep as a family's bond. Perfect for fans of found family, rainbow-hued hope, and resolutions that lead to brighter, bolder tomorrows—because in Willow Creek, every murmur holds the promise of light.

Chapter 1

The fairy lights strung across Sunnybrook Cottage Daycare's porch twinkled like captured stars, casting a soft glow over the fading anniversary party. Laughter swelled and waned from inside, a chorus of parents swapping stories while children chased fireflies in the garden. Theresa Daye-Reed had stepped out for a breath of fresh air, the warm breeze whispering through Willow Creek's misty valleys. It was a night to celebrate ten years of glitter, giggles, and growth. And the quiet victory of a community that had chosen light over lurking shadows.

As she reached up to straighten a sagging string of lights, her fingers brushed something tucked underneath them. A plain white envelope—no stamp, no return address, just her name in tightly drawn block letters. Her pulse quickened, echoes of past anonymous notes flashing through her mind, of shadows in drawings and various dangers unraveling. She opened it and read the few words inside, then slipped it into her pocket, forcing a smile as Alex called from the doorway.

"Ready to head home, love? Emily's got her backpack of art supplies, plus something she's declaring 'protector shadow central.'"

Theresa nodded, pushing the envelope's weight from her thoughts. "Let's go. Mia and Javi can handle the final cleanup."

The drive home was filled with Emily's chatter about the party's highlights. From her perspective, it was Leon's firefly drawings, Janey's paper whirligig, and Milo's "rawr" during the bubble chase. But once they arrived at the Maple Street house, routine took over. Bath time for Emily, with bubbles shaped like friendly monsters, then bedtime stories from *The Day the Crayons Quit*, Alex's voice rising and falling in dramatic flair.

Later, Theresa sipped decaf chamomile tea with Alex in the living room, the note burning a hole in her pocket. She tried to forget it, focusing on his excited ramble about bookstore renovations.

Not tonight, she thought, kissing him good night. *Tomorrow's soon enough for mysteries.*

***

Morning arrived with the familiar uneasy nausea that had first signaled their pregnancy. It was a secret they'd kept close for weeks, savoring it like a whispered promise. Theresa nibbled on saltine crackers from the nightstand, chasing them with flat lemon-lime soda water, the combo that had become her tummy-saving ritual. She whispered a quick prayer to whatever deity oversaw expectant mothers: "Please, just let me not yark in the car."

The queasiness ebbed enough for her to shuffle to the closet, where the laundry basket waited. Fishing out yesterday's sundress, she retrieved the envelope from its pocket.

Her name stared back in those stark letters. Heart pounding, she opened it, unfolding the single sheet inside.

The note was brief, but even the second read-through carried enough weight to alter Theresa's breathing patterns.

"My daughter's whispers are too quiet.

Bonnie draws things she shouldn't know.

Please help."

No signature. Just a phone number scrawled at the bottom.

Theresa sank onto the edge of the bed, staring at the words. *Whispers? Drawings of impossible things?* It echoed the cryptic pleas that had upended their lives before, events filled with shadows, mazes, and even hidden dangers. *How many more secrets could Willow Creek hold?*

She didn't know how long she'd been sitting there, lost in thought, when Alex walked in, two mugs of decaf tea steaming in his hands. His easy smile faded as he took in her expression, then the note. Setting the mugs down, he sat beside her, reading over her shoulder. She watched as his face cycled through emotions, from anger at the intrusion, to intrigue at the puzzle, and finally, a flicker of fear she rarely saw on his steady features.

"Another one," he said quietly, his hand covering hers. "We don't have to dive in. Not with everything going on."

Theresa leaned into him, the warmth of his presence grounding her. "But if we don't, who will? It's a child, Alex. Whispers too quiet and drawings she shouldn't know."

He nodded, fear giving way to resolve. "Together, then. But carefully. I vote we go with Team Reed first in mind. We protect each other, and the things we love."

***

The nausea lingered as Theresa made her slow way to the kitchen, the unwelcome scent of cinnamon oatmeal wafting through the air. Emily sat at the table with Alex, both looking up with matching expressions of nerves. Emily's face was pale, and Alex's forehead was sweaty despite the cool morning.

Theresa opened the fridge, grabbing another lemon-lime soda. She cracked it open, taking a tiny sip that settled her stomach, then a larger one. Turning back, she found them staring. "What?"

"Are you dying?" Emily blurted, her voice overlapping Alex's hurried "Emily has some questions."

"Sorry," came their perfectly synced apologies, and Theresa bit back a chuckle.

"No, I'm not dying. I'm not even ill." She demonstrated with another sip, the fizz calming her further.

"Then what's wrong with you?" Emily asked. "I've heard you getting sick every morning. People who are dying are sick a lot."

"Have you ever met a person who was actively dying to make that blanket statement?" Theresa took her seat at the corner table, across from Emily and beside Alex. "Because there's a lot of supposition there."

"Well, no. But I asked Delphinia, and she said her grandma was sick all the time before she died." Emily's fingers twirled a colored pencil like a fidget toy, her chin dipping. "I told her I was worried about you."

"And what did Delphinia say then?" She was an older child who sometimes came to the daycare with her little sister. Delphinia was old enough to babysit her sister on her own, but she wanted the security of still having adults around.

Tone sullen, Emily made air quotes. "'It's important to communicate.' Which I know, all right? I know that. I just was…I don't know."

"Scared?" Theresa reached out, covering Emily's hand. "I get that. If you were sick every morning but hadn't told me, I'd be afraid."

"Yeah."

Alex's foot pressed against Theresa's under the table, a silent anchor. "I didn't want to get ahead of anything you had planned," he said.

"See? What does that even mean?" Emily asked loudly. "Why can't you just tell me, Daddy A?"

"Because it's news for the whole family. And fortunately, we all appear to be present and attentive right now." Theresa drew in a slow breath, her heartbeat quickening. "We're adding to our family, Emily. We don't know if it's a boy or a girl yet, but we'll become a family of four in about five months."

"What?"

"Momma T is expecting. She's pregnant. We're pregnant," Alex explained.

"A baby? You're not dying?" The disbelief in Emily's voice made Theresa grin. "We're having a baby?"

Just like that, the worry she'd been carrying was whisked away. "Yeah, Em. We're having a baby."

"Will we know if it's a witchling or a warlockling?"

Alex stepped in smoothly. "Yes, at an upcoming appointment in a few weeks. You could even go if you wanted. You could check out the tech and talk to the person doing the ultrasound."

They chatted for a few more minutes, excitement bubbling. Then Emily declared, "I need to draw everything in my head right now!" She jumped up, ran out, then dashed back for a gentle hug. "We're having a baby." And then she was gone again.

Theresa grinned. "And just like that, Emily's on board with Team Baby."

"'Warlockling' is a new one," Alex said, humor in his voice. "I don't hate it, though."

***

At dinner that night, Emily presented Theresa and Alex with a drawing of their growing family. It was more basic than a lot of her art—she'd done them as stick figures under a rainbow, the baby a shadowy outline waiting to be colored.

"I left the baby a shadow so I can fill them in once we know which flavor we're getting." Her reasoning was so pragmatic it made Theresa grin. "And if it's a witchling, it's gotta be witchling two. Cuz I'm witchling one."

Alex had his head down, studying a piece of paper next to his plate. Theresa leaned over, lifting his chin. "Hey, there you are."

"I'm sorry. I'm just angsting over which shelving to buy. It feels like everything from the flooring to the shelving will set the tone for the store, and I want to pick correctly." He offered her the paper. "It's a toss-up between quality and quantity, quality or size. Like that old joke about websites—which I'm going to need, too, by the way. You can have a site coded cheap and fast, but not good; or fast and good, but not cheap; or cheap and good, but not fast. Or something like that."

"Have you narrowed down a name yet?"

"Everything I've thought of is bad—like dad-joke bad."

"Why don't you just call it Reed Between the Lines?" Emily speared a piece of broccoli, waving it like a wand. "That's got your name, and it means reading too."

"Has my name?"

Theresa slapped the table. "Reed Between the Lines. Witchling, you're a genius."

Alex tilted his head, and Emily laughed.

"Alex Reed Between the Lines, but without the Alex part," she explained.

His mouth opened slowly, eyes widening with joy. "Reed. Reed Between the Lines. That's perfect, Em. Thank you."

She waved the broccoli again. "Good thing I work cheap. You can pay me in books."

Theresa laughed and passed the paper back. "Get shelves no more than six feet tall. You don't want it to feel like library stacks. Go with the light honey finish; that should reflect the overhead lights without obnoxious glaring."

"Easy as that?" Alex chuckled, jotting notes before folding the paper under his plate. "I should come to you with all my questions."

"As long as we can do it together, I believe there's all kinds of things we can do." Theresa smiled at her husband. "I love you, Mr. Reed."

"I love you, Mrs. Daye-Reed."

"And I love you both." Emily tucked the broccoli into her mouth, chewing fast. "And I love the baby already. I can't wait."

***

The next morning, the daily dance of nausea continued. Theresa nibbled her crackers, sipped her lemon-lime soda water, and slowly brought her uneasy stomach under control. "Please, just let me not yark in the car."

Alex was already out the door by the time she reached the kitchen. He had planned on stopping by the storefront to measure for shelving, given their new height restrictions.

"Come on, witchling. We need to get going."

"I'm already ready." Emily walked past with a smile. "Daddy A made me oatmeal again this morning. He said it might be easier if he and I had breakfast without you, since your tummy's an unhappy camper."

"Daddy A would be correct." Theresa grabbed a protein shake from the fridge. "From waking until about now, my tummy is definitely unhappy."

"Why is that?" Emily swung into the back seat, buckling her booster. "That seems like a dumb thing."

"I agree. I should be able to eat everything I want. I'm growing a whole new human."

"Whoa. I didn't think about that." Emily went silent, and Theresa glanced in the mirror to see her biting her bottom lip.

"Yup, a baby is all of that." Theresa pulled in beside the cottage, putting the car in Park. "Ready to be creative today?"

"Yes, ma'am. Oh, are we secret-keeping?"

"Are we what?" Theresa gathered her shake, purse, and beach-bag-sized tote, then opened her door.

"Does Miss Mia know about the b-a-b-y?"

"Does Miss Mia know about the *what*?" The screech came from beside the car.

Theresa looked back at Emily, whose eyes were wide.

"I'm sorry," she mouthed, and Theresa smiled.

"No damage done, witchling." Hands closed around her arm, tugging her free so fast she nearly dropped everything. "Easy there, hoss." Mia was smiling, her eyes asking the question. "Yes, we're pregnant."

Mia started jumping up and down, joined by Emily.

"If you don't stop jerking me around, I might yark." Mia stopped jumping but kept rising on her toes. "You're the second person we've told, so zip ya lip."

"We're excited." Emily laughed, grabbing Mia's hands for a new jumping celebration, this one at least without involving Theresa. "So excited, Miss Mia."

The morning unfolded in its familiar rhythm, with greetings and hand-offs at the rainbow door, cubbies filled with backward coats—which, according to kid logic, turned the sleeves into wings—and the brass bell chiming for circle time. Theresa led the group, her voice steady despite the lingering queasiness. "Good morning, friends!"

"Good morning, Miss T!" they chorused, Milo adding his signature "Rawr!"

As they settled into sharing time, little Janey Simmon raised her hand, then leaned over to whisper in Priya's ear, too quiet for the group, but Priya's eyes widened.

"Janey, sweetie, want to share with everyone?" Theresa encouraged gently.

Janey shook her head, whispering again, this time to the air, as if confiding in an invisible friend. "The whispers say...the river knows secrets."

The room went quiet, a chill prickling Theresa's arms. *Whispers? Secrets?* It echoed the note too closely, like a child's innocent murmur foreshadowing the mystery ahead.

Theresa recovered with a smile. "Whispers can be fun, like secret games. Let's talk about our favorite secrets. Like hidden rainbows!"

But as the circle continued, Janey's words lingered, a faint echo in the wind.

That night, Theresa reclined against pillows on the couch, laptop propped on her legs. She was working on the *Kid Quips* blog post, titling it *Whispers and Wonders.*

"Hey Quipsters,

Circle-time magic: One little one leans in and murmurs, 'The whispers say...the river knows secrets.' Innocent imagination or a peek into hidden worlds? Either way, it sparked a rainbow hunt!

Tips keep our exits bright—thank you!

—Miss T"

Theresa set the blog to post on a schedule, then opened a new browser window. Casually, she searched for the best colors to achieve retail sales, surprised when she actually received results.

Alex walked into the room, and she waved him over.

"Look at this. Isn't that crazy? They've studied colors in retail. I knew they'd done research for fast-food places, where yellow and red are used a lot because those colors tend to move people along faster. I guess I shouldn't be surprised the marketing people in the world had done the same for stores."

"What color do they recommend for bookstores?" Alex lifted Theresa's feet and put them on his lap, turning to face her as he started rubbing her feet and ankles.

"A subtle cream or the lightest green I've ever seen." She tipped her head to one side. "What color did we pick?"

"We picked a subtle cream for the main walls and a light pistachio green for the checkout area." He laughed, digging into her arch with his thumb. "It's like we're intelligent or something."

"Emily would say it was the 'or something' comment."

"She's such a great kid, T. We're so lucky to have her."

"Yes, we are." Theresa hummed. "You're putting me to sleep, Alex."

"Then let's motor over to the bedroom and put ourselves to sleep for real." He took her legs from his lap and placed her feet on the floor. Standing, he held out a hand to help her up, and Theresa didn't hesitate to reach out and grab hold. Alex put an arm around her shoulders and Theresa slipped hers around his waist, and together they made their way to bed.

***

The next night found them back in the living room, brainstorming more bookstore details. Theresa watched as Alex erased another sketch of the store's layout.

"Can I recommend something?"

"Please, save me from myself here, T."

"Look at this." She brought out the tablet where she'd already loaded a software she'd used when planning out the daycare. "We tell it how many shelves, the size of the space, if one space is primary or something. This was a lifesaver when we were working on the cottage." She demonstrated how to use it, then handed it over to Alex. He took it wordlessly, already intent on the device.

"I think we should have a themed event every month," she continued. "Some of them will be easy, like Valentine's Day, but some months would be a little different, like May. That could be the lead-up to school being off for the summer."

"We could do a display for books for mothers." He tilted his head and gave her a grin. "Or mothers-to-be."

"I wish there was an actual handbook for mothers-to-be. That would make my life easier, for sure."

"What are you worried about?" Alex was looking back at the tablet as he moved shelving around on the screen. "You're already a professional caretaker. Our baby won't want for anything."

"I'm worried about working and being a mom. I know I'm already doing that with Emily, but a baby's different. Their entire existence depends on adult humans doing the right thing at the right time." She shrugged. "What if I miss something critical? No one to blame but myself."

Alex's head lifted until he was staring her in the face. "Where are these doubts coming from, T?"

"From reality. Already the morning sickness has impacted my ability to do necessary things. It seems like Mia's having to pick up more responsibilities every day. What if she gets tired of pulling more than her weight and leaves the cottage?"

"Mia's not going anywhere. That isn't even on the radar, so what's really bothering you?" He reached out and wrapped an arm around her shoulders, bringing her back to lean against him. "Tell Daddy A. Let me take some of that worry load from you."

"How do people balance baby, job, and home life? That's the thing that bugs me the most. How do people effortlessly do this thing that already feels overwhelming?"

"Why do you think it's effortless? I was talking to one of the ladies at the library the other day. She told me she worried about parentifying her older child with a new baby. With work, she didn't see another solution but to have her twelve-year-old pick up some of the time with the baby. I reminded her that there was a nursery over at the church that kept the cost reasonable. She hadn't thought about taking the baby to a daycare. Within a few minutes, she'd signed up for the service, then called the school to tell them her older daughter could take advantage of the after-school tutoring her teachers had recommended."

"Sounds like you helped a lot. I don't think taking my child to another daycare is something I'd pursue, though," Theresa told him.

"So take them to the cottage."

She shook her head. "We have a hard age limit starting at three years old. We're not set up or licensed for infants or smaller toddlers."

"So change the setup and get licensed. If you start now, you'll have it under control by the time you need it."

"Just like that?"

"No, it'll take work to get everything ready, but you've got a wonderful husband willing to hire a handyman to help with any redesign or construction." He laughed. "Don't expect me to swing a hammer, though."

"I won't." She paused for a beat, then said, "It means more than you know that you're willing to listen."

"Then I'll promise to always listen, T. Not to whispers or echoes, but just you."

Chapter 2

Heading into the last day of the workweek, Theresa sat in the car and stared at the note one last time before pulling out her phone, her thumb hovering over the keypad. The phone number stared back, a string of digits that could unravel another thread in Willow Creek's tapestry of secrets. Alex had urged caution, meaning "Text first, then meet in public," and she agreed. With the pregnancy adding a brand-new layer to his protectiveness, she wasn't about to dive in blindly.

Coffee at Maple Café tomorrow, 10 a.m.? Let's talk about your daughter. Theresa Daye-Reed.

The reply came almost instantly: *Yes. Thank you. Tamika Sullivan.*

Theresa exhaled, pocketing her phone. Tamika Sullivan was a new name, and it seemed only fitting that she'd bring a new mystery. But as Theresa made her way into the daycare, the whispers in the note lingered like fog off the river.

***

The Maple Café buzzed with midmorning weekend energy, the aroma of lavender lattes and cinnamon scones a comforting constant in Willow Creek. Theresa arrived early, claiming a corner booth with a view of Main Street. She ordered a decaf latte, her hand absently resting on her belly, a reminder of new life amid old enigmas. Pregnancy fatigue tugged at the edges of her energy, but curiosity helped sharpen her focus.

Tamika Sullivan pushed through the door exactly on time, looking somewhat harried and hurried. Her auburn hair was actively escaping a messy bun on top of her head, and she had a large tote slung over one shoulder. She looked mid-thirties, dressed in practical jeans and a sweater, the kind of mom who balanced work calls with playground runs. Trailing her was a small girl Theresa assumed was Bonnie. She appeared to be about six years old, with wide blue eyes and a sketchbook clutched like a shield. Bonnie's gaze darted around, as if looking to source the overlapping voices in the store.

"Theresa?" Tamika spotted her, weaving through tables. "Thank you for meeting us. I'm Tamika, and this is Bonnie."

Theresa stood, offering a warm smile. "Of course. Please, sit. Lavender latte? It's the house special."

Tamika nodded gratefully, ordering one for herself and a hot cocoa for Bonnie. As the barista bustled away, Tamika leaned in, her voice low. "We're new here. We just moved from Eugene a month ago for a fresh start. Job transfer, you know? But Bonnie…" She slipped an arm around her daughter's shoulders. "She's told me that something's wrong. I believe her. Bonnie whispers things, faint like echoes, and her drawings…" She twisted in her seat and pulled a folder from her tote, sliding it across the table.

Theresa opened it carefully. The sketches were childish but precise. She was looking at crayon scenes recreating a segment of Willow Creek's history that no six-year-old should know. Especially one not even from the area. The first picture in the pile depicted a fire at the old Whitaker Mill, flames licking wooden beams, workers fleeing in panic. That had happened back in the 1920s, well before the mill was rebuilt a decade later. Another showed underground tunnels snaking beneath the town, water dripping from stone walls. A third had a group of figures huddled by the river, their mouths open in silent screams, labeled in wobbly letters, "The whispers say help."

A chill prickled Theresa's skin. "These are very detailed. Has she studied local history?"

Tamika shook her head, eyes glistening. "No. We haven't even visited the town museum. She draws them after…well, all I know to call them is her 'whispering fits.' It's like she's hearing voices. Like she's listening to something far away, very faint, murmuring. I took her to doctors, medical doctors. They've all said it's imagination or anxiety from the move, but I know it's more. Your blog, *Kid Quips*, it mentioned helping kids with 'wrong' drawings before. Please, can you help?"

Bonnie, quiet until now, looked up from her cocoa. She leaned toward Theresa, her voice a bare whisper, as if pulled from thinning air. "The river remembers there was a fire in the dark, and then there were whispers in the walls." The words faded like wind, echoing slightly, unnaturally. Bonnie blinked, then smiled innocently. "Can I have a cookie?"

Theresa's heart raced. Bonnie's whispers weren't just faint, but they also held an otherworldly timbre, like voices carried on a breeze. She nodded at Tamika. "We'll figure this out. Together."

As they wrapped up, Theresa's mind whirled. *Historical scenes Bonnie shouldn't know that are tied to the mill? The river?* It felt like Willow Creek's past was murmuring back.

***

The next day, Theresa looked up the local museum online and saw they were open half days on Sundays. Something drew her to the idea of doing a little research of her own.

"Alex, I think I'm going to visit the Willow Creek Museum. Want to go with me?" She peered around the doorframe back into the living room. Alex had spreadsheets laid on the coffee table in front of him. "Might make a good distraction from the demands of opening a new bookstore."

"I shouldn't. If I can get this order in by tomorrow morning, I'll be able to use the publisher's discount code for the month. That promotion ends at noon." Shaking his head, he looked up at her, frown lines between furrowed brows. "I'm just looking to trim expenses anywhere I can."

"Don't they do a discount every month?" She walked out and sat next to him. "Is it truly time sensitive?"

"They do different discounts. This month it's 40 percent off wholesale on textbooks. They include a variety of self-help books in the textbook category." He shrugged. "Next month it might be 10 percent off comic books."

"Ah, gotta strike while the iron's hot. I get it. Okay, do your work, and I shall go wander among the artistry that is Willow Creek." Raising her voice, she called, "Emily, want to go to the local museum with me?"

"Can't," came from Emily's bedroom. "I've got homework."

"So studious," Theresa called back. "I'll go by myself, then," she said to Alex.

"What about Mia? Can she go with you?" He didn't look up as he made the recommendation.

"I didn't think about that. I'll give her a call from the car."

Theresa stepped out into the crisp Sunday afternoon air, the sun filtering through the canopy of maples that lined their quiet street. There was a sense of history in Willow Creek that lingered like morning mist. But today, something tugged at her, an itch to uncover more about the whispers she'd heard in passing from locals. The mill fire from decades ago.

She slid into her car, which still smelled faintly of the vanilla air freshener Emily insisted was the only scent she could bear, and pulled out her phone to call Mia.

The line rang twice before Mia picked up, her voice bursting through the speaker like a confetti cannon. "Theresa! My favorite boss lady! What's the haps? Are you calling to bail me out of my thrilling afternoon of reorganizing my spice rack?"

Theresa chuckled. "Actually, the opposite. I'm heading to the Willow Creek Museum for a little history dive. Want to tag along? Alex is buried in spreadsheets, and Emily's got homework. I could use some company. Preferably the kind that makes me laugh instead of yawn."

"Museum? On a Sunday? Girl, you know how to party." They shared a laugh. "But sure, why not? I've got nothing better to do than alphabetize cumin and turmeric. Pick me up in ten? I'll bring snacks. Museum food is always overpriced worse than theater popcorn."

"Deal. See you soon."

Theresa hung up, a smile tugging at her lips. Mia had a type of infectious energy, the perfect antidote to the mild fatigue that had been creeping in lately. She'd found that pregnancy was a sneaky thing. Her mornings were slowly becoming better, but now, by midday, her body reminded her it was building a tiny human. She rubbed her belly absentmindedly as she drove the short distance to Mia's house, a colorful Victorian conversion on the edge of downtown.

Mia was waiting on the stoop, waving dramatically with a reusable tote bag slung over her shoulder. She hopped into the car, her curly hair bouncing like springs. "All right, history buff, what's the real reason? You digging for dirt on that old mill fire? I heard whispers—pun intended—about your visit at the coffee shop yesterday."

Theresa merged onto Main Street, the road winding past shops with faded awnings. "Wow. Gossip travels fast."

"Javi heard it from someone who heard it from someone. They thought you might be interviewing someone, but said something looked sus."

"Not an interview, but more of a concerning conversation about a note we got. Tamika Sullivan and her daughter, Bonnie. They moved here recently. I've been curious about the town's past. Feels like there's more to Willow Creek than meets the eye." She shook her head. "Side note: She might bring Bonnie by to do a trial day soon. Sweet kiddo, will mesh well with our existing group."

"Good to know." Mia rummaged in her bag and pulled out a granola bar, offering one to Theresa. "Well, if we're time-traveling via artifacts, count me in for comic relief. I'll be the one asking if the dinosaurs ate at the mill cafeteria."

The museum was a modest two-story building on the outskirts of town, a converted schoolhouse from the 1800s with weathered brick walls and a sign that creaked in the breeze: "Willow Creek Historical Society—Unveiling the Past." They parked in the nearly empty lot, gravel crunching under the tires.

As they approached the entrance, Theresa felt a wave of tiredness wash over her, her legs a bit heavier than usual. She paused, taking a deep breath. This was growth, she reminded herself. She had to start learning to listen to her body, not push through like she was used to doing.

Mia noticed and linked arms with her. "You okay? Not museum-phobic, are you?"

"Just a little pooped. Pregnancy perk number 47: I get random energy dips that can lead to amazing naps." Theresa smiled weakly. "But I'm good. Let's do this."

"Ohh, I remember that. Hard pass."

Inside, the air was thick with the scent of polished wood. The floors groaned under their footsteps, each creak echoing like a whisper from the past. Dim light filtered through tall, narrow windows, casting long beams of light over glass cases filled with dusty exhibits. Arrowheads from indigenous settlements, faded photographs of loggers down by the river, and rusted tools from the early days of the pre-fire and post-fire mill lined the walls. A small sign at the front desk read "Admission, $5 Suggested Donation," with a jar half filled with crumpled bills.

Behind the desk sat the curator, a wiry man in his late sixties with a shock of white hair and glasses perched on the end of his nose. He looked up from a yellowed ledger, his eyes lighting up like he'd just discovered a lost artifact. "Welcome, ladies! I'm Nathan Barrows, keeper of Willow Creek's secrets. First-time visitors?"

Theresa nodded, dropping a ten into the jar. "Yes, we're interested in the town's history, especially around the time period of the old mill fire."

Nathan's face brightened further, if that was possible. He adjusted his glasses and leaned forward conspiratorially. "Ah, the Great Blaze of '23. A pivotal moment! It nearly destroyed the heart of our economy but birthed a thousand legends. Follow me, ladies. I believe I've got just the exhibit."

Mia whispered to Theresa as they trailed him, "He looks like he time-traveled from a steampunk convention. Bet he sleeps in a coffin lined with history books."

Nathan led them to a corner room labeled "Industrial Era Tragedies." The space was dimly lit, with spotlights illuminating curated charred remnants of the fire, including a twisted metal gear from the mill's machinery, a singed worker's cap, and a glass case holding a leather-bound journal. Dust motes danced in the beams of light, and the air felt cooler here, almost chilled. Theresa's footsteps echoed on the creaky oak floors, each one a reminder of this building's age.

"Here we are," Nathan announced, gesturing grandly. "The survivor's journal. Belonged to one Jeremiah Cobb, a foreman who escaped the flames. His entries can be haunting." He unlocked the case with a key from his pocket and carefully opened the journal to a marked page, yellowed and brittle.

Theresa leaned in, her eyes scanning the faded ink. The writing was spidery, urgently slanting forward. She read it aloud. "April 15, 1923. The whispers started weeks ago. Faint at first, like wind through the cracks. But tonight, as the fire took hold, they grew louder. Voices in the smoke, calling names, urging us deeper into the blaze. I fled, but others...they listened. God help their souls."

A shiver ran down Theresa's spine, unrelated to the room's draft. *Whispers.* Just like the rumors she'd overheard. She straightened, feeling a twinge in her lower back from bending over. The fatigue was settling in deeper, a gentle fog at the edges of her mind.

Mia peered over her shoulder, munching on a granola bar crumb. "Whispers? Sounds like a bad horror movie. Or maybe the mill workers were just hearing the river. You know, that cursed river stone legend?"

Nathan perked up at that, closing and returning the journal to the display with reverence. "Ah, you've heard of the Whispering Stones! A campfire tale if ever there was one." He shuffled to a nearby pedestal, where a smooth gray river rock sat under glass, etched with faint runes that looked suspiciously modern. "Legend says that stones like this one, pulled from the creek bed in

1890, amplify sounds. Place it near water, and you'll hear echoes of the past, be they ghostly voices or whispered lost secrets. Some say it cursed the mill, making workers hear things that weren't there. But between you and me?" He winked. "It's probably just a fancy echo effect from the minerals. Tourists love it, though. Want to hold it? For luck?"

Mia grinned. "Heck yeah! If it amplifies sounds, maybe it'll make my singing voice better." She reached out as Nathan handed it over, careful not to drop it. "Ooh, it's heavy. Hey, Theresa, say something profound so I can test it."

Theresa laughed, but it came out softer than intended. The room was spinning just a touch—not dizziness, but that pregnant exhaustion where everything felt a beat slower. "How about 'Mia, don't break the cursed rock'?"

Mia held it to her ear dramatically. "Nothing. Wait. I hear...the sound of my own bad decisions!" She handed it back to Nathan, who chuckled.

As they wandered the exhibits, Nathan regaled them with more folklore, from tales of river spirits that lured fishermen to the "echo bridge" where shouts returned as whispers.

Red herrings, Theresa thought. *Distractions from the real history*. But the journal entry stuck with her. *Whispers urging people into the fire. Was it delirium from smoke inhalation? Or something more?*

They moved to a display of photographs of black-and-white images from the mill pre-fire, workers posing with somber expressions, and then of the post-blaze ruins, with charred beams jutting like bones. The museum's creaky floors seemed louder here, each step a protest. Dust tickled Theresa's nose, and she sneezed softly, waving away Mia's concerned look.

"You sure you're okay? We can bail if you need a nap," Mia said, lowering her voice as Nathan drifted to help another visitor—a lone elderly man examining arrowheads.

"I'm fine. You know how it is. For some reason, growing a whole new person takes energy."

Theresa sat on a nearby bench, the wood warming underneath her touch. She closed her eyes briefly, breathing in the museum's quiet. This fatigue was a teacher, forcing her to slow down, to reflect. Before, she would have powered through deadlines on coffee and adrenaline. Now she was learning patience. With the town, with Alex's bookstore struggles, and even with herself. It was personal growth, coming all wrapped up in discomfort.

Mia plopped down beside her. "Pregnancy is absolutely a full-time job. I remember the tiredness very well. Milo sapped me of energy like water draining from a bucket with a hole in it." She leaned her head back, then said, "Oh, hey, look at this." She pointed to the wall, reading from a sign, "The mill fire claimed twenty-three lives, but survivors spoke of unnatural phenomena.

Investigations blamed faulty wiring, but whispers persist."

"Whispers again," Theresa murmured. "It's like the town's built on them."

Nathan returned, carrying a small booklet. "If you're keen on the fire, take this pamphlet. I compiled it myself, and it includes maps of the old mill site, from before it was rebuilt in the '30s. There remain some ruins visible down by the river. Folks say you can still hear echoes there on quiet nights."

"Thanks. I've been to the old mill. It certainly carries the weight of history," Theresa said, tucking the leaflet into her purse.

As they thanked him and headed out, the sun was dipping lower, casting golden hues over the parking lot. Her steps felt lighter now, the rest having helped. Mia chattered about dinner plans, but Theresa's mind lingered on the journal.

Back in the car, Mia buckled up. "That was fun. Creepy, but fun. You think those whispers were real? Or just mass hysteria?"

Theresa started the engine, glancing at the museum in the rearview. "I don't know. But I want to find out more. Maybe visit the mill site again."

"As long as I bring the cursed rock for backup," Mia quipped.

They drove off, laughter filling the car, but Theresa felt a subtle shift inside, a curiosity blooming alongside her child, urging her to uncover Willow Creek's hidden voices.

Theresa's phone buzzed in her cupholder. It was Alex. She answered on speaker. "Hey, how's the spreadsheet war going?"

"Victorious. Order placed. How was the museum? Find any buried treasure?"

Mia leaned in. "Just a cursed rock that makes you hear ghosts. No biggie."

Alex laughed. "Sounds like a typical Sunday in Willow Creek. Pick up milk on your way home? Emily's dead set on having cereal for supper."

"Will do. See you soon."

Theresa hung up, navigating the winding road back toward town. The river glinted to their left, a silver ribbon under the afternoon light.

"You know, Mia, that journal got me thinking. What if the whispers weren't just imagination? The town has this vibe."

Mia nodded, unwrapping another granola bar. "Vibe? Like, haunted vibe? I've lived here my whole life, and yeah, there's been some weird stuff. But it mostly tracks back to solid reality. Remember that time the bridge lights flickered during the storm? Folks said it was spirits. Turned out to be squirrels chewing wires."

"But the mill fire—twenty-three people dead. That's not nothing." Theresa's voice softened as another wave of fatigue hit. She gripped the wheel tighter, focusing on the road. Pregnancy was teaching her limits, but also resilience. She wasn't the type to back down from a mystery.

Theresa waved goodbye to Mia from the car window as she dropped her off, the house's colorful door swinging shut behind her friend. The drive to the store and then home was thankfully short, the warm weight in her limbs making her grateful for the familiar route. Willow Creek's streets were quiet on Sundays, the kind of quiet that amplified every rustle of leaves or distant dog bark. She pulled into the driveway, grabbed the milk from the passenger seat, and let herself in through the side door.

Alex looked up from the kitchen table, where his spreadsheets had migrated. "Successful mission?"

"Very." She put the milk in the fridge and joined him, peeking at his screen. Rows of numbers swam before her eyes—inventory, costs, projections. "Mia was a riot, as usual. The curator was this quirky guy who spun tales like a spider builds webs."

"Sounds entertaining. Find anything interesting on the mill?"

"Yeah, a survivor's journal. Mentioned whispers during the fire." She hesitated, not wanting to sound too invested. Alex was practical. She knew he'd chalk it up to folklore.

He nodded absently, typing. "Whispers? Like hallucinations from smoke inhalation?"

"Maybe. But it was eerie." She rubbed her temples, a mild headache from the dusty air lingering. Pregnancy fatigue wasn't just physical; she'd found it toyed with her focus, reminding her to prioritize. No more all-nighters allowed. This was her growth, embracing the slow, the steady.

Emily wandered in, hair in a messy bun, homework notebook in hand. "Museum fun?"

"It was cool. Old artifacts, creaky everything." Theresa smiled. "You should've come—there was a cursed rock."

"Cursed how?"

"Supposedly amplifies sounds, makes you hear ghosts or something. The curator let Mia hold it."

Emily's eyes lit up. "For real? Did it work?"

"Nah, just a rock." But as Theresa said it, she wondered. The journal's words echoed in her mind: *Voices in the smoke, calling names.*

That night, as she lay in bed beside Alex, the house settling with its own creaks, she couldn't sleep. The pamphlet from Nathan sat on her nightstand. She flipped on the lamp, careful not to wake Alex, and read. Maps of the mill site, survivor accounts, newspaper clippings from 1923. One article caught her eye: "Mystery Sounds Preceded Blaze—Workers Report Unearthly Whispers."

****

The next morning, Theresa woke with renewed energy. Pregnancy had its ups and downs—today was beginning on an up.

But by midday, the fatigue hit like a wave crashing over the daycare's rainbow rug. Circle time had been a success. Emily's "baby prep" ideas sparked kid drawings of families with shadowy siblings, but Theresa's energy plummeted. The nausea had passed, but exhaustion clung like glitter after a craft explosion.

Mia noticed immediately, her co-director's intuition sharp as ever. "Boss, you look like you wrestled a dino and lost. Go home and take a nap in your own bed. I've got this."

Theresa hesitated, glancing at the playroom where kids buzzed with activity. "You sure? The twins are on a tear today."

Mia waved her off, crayon still tucked in her bun. "Positive. Jasmine's leading song time, and I've got Milo on block duty. Nap now, conquer later."

Grateful, Theresa drove home, sinking onto their comfortable couch. She set a twenty-minute alarm before sleep claimed her quickly, dreams swirling with faint whispers and crayon flames.

She woke to a soft kiss on her cheek, opening her eyes to see Alex sitting back. "Mia said you were feeling like a nap."

"I don't know why, but exhaustion just hit me like a ton of bricks." She glanced at the clock, sitting up and swinging her legs off the couch. "I thought I'd set an alarm."

"It was still going off when I came in. I shut it down, figuring I had a much more pleasant way to wake you." He waggled his eyebrows ridiculously, and Theresa gave him the laughter he was looking for. "Did it work?"

"Well, I am awake." Theresa leaned sideways, resting her head on his shoulder. "I should go back to the cottage."

"I'm headed back to the library in a few minutes. Want me to drive you? I get off before pickup time, so I can come over and help with cleanup."

"Oh, that would be great," she said with a sigh. "I can't wait for the pregnancy cycle where I have tons of energy."

Alex dropped her off, and she walked through the back door of the cottage, hearing giggling just inside. Peeking in, she found Emily at a low table, surrounded by a cluster of kids, guiding art time. At ten, Emily was a natural. Her braid swung as she demonstrated. "See? Draw the baby with a heart, like a protector shadow. That's for love!"

Priya nodded solemnly. "My baby sister needs rainbows, too, for feelings bridges."

Milo added with a roar, "And dinos! For guarding the crib. Rawr!"

Theresa smiled, the fatigue lifting slightly. Emily spotted her, waving a drawing. "Momma T! Look, we're helping Priya's new baby sister!"

Mia sidled up, whispering, "Kid's a pro. Told her it had to be a surprise project. She promised no leaks."

Theresa hugged Emily close. "Perfect, witchling. You've got such great ideas."

As the day wound on, the whispers from the note echoed in her mind—but with her family's light, they felt less daunting. Still, Tamika and Bonnie needed help.

Time to dig deeper.

She sat with Alex at the kitchen table, him working on organizing all the non-book things needed for a bookstore, and her working on a new *Kid Quips* blog post, *Art Time Whispers.*

"Hey Quipsters,

Art time whispers: One kiddo leans in, says, 'My baby sister needs rainbows for feelings bridges.' Another roars, 'And dinos! For guarding the crib. Rawr!' Family prep at its finest, with secrets and sparkles included.

Your tips fuel our rainbows—thank you!

—Miss T"

"Want another decaf?" Alex asked, straightening up his papers.

She shook her head. "No, I think I need a warm shower and then bed."

"I'll finish loading the dishwasher. Em got a little sidetracked earlier."

"She's already in bed."

"Which is why I'll finish the job. It's no hardship. Go on." He gave her a little push. "Get your shower. I'll see you in our room in a few minutes."

"Aye, aye, captain." She grinned and kissed him softly. "Love you, Alex."

Chapter 3

The aroma of Alex's homemade lasagna filled the house, a comforting reminder of home after a day of daycare whirlwinds and lingering thoughts of Tamika Sullivan's plea. Theresa set the table. Her movements were deliberate and slow to ward off the fatigue that still nipped at her heels. Emily bounced in, her latest drawing of a "whisper protector" inspired by circle time clutched in one hand, while Alex pulled the dish from the oven, his apron dusted with flour.

"Dinner's served!" Alex announced with flair, plating generous portions. "Extra cheese for the growing Reed team."

They settled in, the clink of forks a rhythmic backdrop. Emily dove into her lasagna, but her eyes darted between her parents. "Momma T, you look...thinky. Is it the baby? Or that meeting at the café?"

Theresa exchanged a glance with Alex, who nodded subtly. They'd agreed to loop Emily in, but she wanted to tread very carefully. At ten, their little girl was perceptive and had experience with devastating loss. But they both knew secrets had a way of whispering louder when hidden.

"Both, witchling," Theresa said, setting down her fork. "Remember the note from the party? I met the mom on Saturday, Tamika Sullivan. She and her daughter, Bonnie, are new to town. Bonnie hears faint whispers and draws things she shouldn't know, like old town history."

Emily's eyes widened. "Whispers? Like Janey's at circle time? 'The river knows secrets'?"

Alex leaned forward, his librarian instincts kicking in. "Exactly like that. I did some digging at the library today, looking for folklore on 'echo hauntings.' Willow Creek's river has stories from back in the 1920s, when the old Whitaker Mill fire trapped workers in underground tunnels. Legends say their voices echo on the wind, like whispers carried from the past. Not ghosts, because I don't believe in them, but maybe it's clever acoustic tricks, with common sounds bouncing off water and stone to build what appears to be supernatural effects."

Theresa shivered despite the warmth in their home. "Bonnie's drawings match that timeframe of fires and tunnels. And her whispers...it's hard to explain, but they sound echoed in real time, faint but clear. Tamika's scared it's something more."

Emily listened intently, then pushed her chair back. "I overheard you talking about it last night. It made me think..." She leaned over and grabbed her sketchbook from the counter, flipping to a new page. As they finished eating, her colored pencils flew, drawing a tall shadow figure, not menacing but swirling with faint lines like sound waves, a heart at its center. "A whisper shadow! It guards secrets but allows good ones to get out, like a friendly echo."

Alex ruffled her hair. "Brilliant, Em. Maybe Bonnie needs one of those."

Theresa smiled, the discussion easing some of her tension. But as they cleared their plates, the note's words ran back through her mind.

She draws things she shouldn't know. What if the river's echoes aren't just legend?

***

"Let's swing by the storefront," Alex suggested after dinner, keys in hand. "I need to visualize those shelves in place, and maybe it'll clear our heads from whisper worries."

They all climbed into the truck, Emily tucked between Theresa and Alex. The drive was short, Willow Creek's streets quiet under the evening lamps. Reed Between the Lines would occupy a charming two-story brick building on Main Street, its windows still papered over during renovations. Alex unlocked the door, flicking on a set of temporary work lights that cast a bright glow over the refinished wood floors.

"Welcome to the future hub of literary adventures," he said, excitement lighting his face. He gestured to the open space. The quality wooden shelves were half installed along one wall, overstuffed chairs scattered like invitations to linger. "Imagine if you will, there will be cozy reading nooks here, a mystery section there with wing chairs, and I thought maybe even a kids' corner with Emily's art on the walls and stuff."

Emily flapped her arms. "So I'd be your bookstore artist? Me?"

"That's what I was thinking, Em." Alex smiled at her while Theresa reached out and pulled him into a hug.

"I've got to go see what I think will work best." Emily was off at a run, angling over to where Alex had pointed.

Theresa wandered around, running her hand over one of the assembled shelves. "It's coming together beautifully. The honey finish was the right call. It feels welcoming, like an extension of the flooring."

But Alex's brow furrowed as he checked a clipboard. "Yeah, but delays are going to be hard to work around. The contractor says he's found unexpected old wiring issues upstairs. That'll push the grand opening back two weeks. And the website guy's quoting double for rush coding." He sighed, tension creeping in. "I want it perfect, you know? For us, for the town."

Theresa stepped closer, wrapping her arms around him. "It will be. You're building something special. This is our next chapter." As she spoke, a soft flutter stirred in her belly, like a whisper from within. She gasped, her hand flying to the spot. "Alex. Oh, I felt it. The first kick."

His eyes widened, fears forgotten as he placed his hand over hers. "Really? Our little one?"

They stood there, the empty store echoing their quiet joy, until another faint kick confirmed it. "Strong already," Theresa whispered. "Like their big sister."

Alex kissed her forehead. "Team Reed, expanding. Whispers and all, we'll handle it." He looked around the room with a satisfied expression on his face. "Em, come on. We're going to head home."

"Did you know there are like three big walls over there where you said the kids' corner would be? That's a lotta art. And it can't be just any art—it's gotta be good. Like art camp good, Daddy A." Emily was talking before she'd even taken a step in their direction.

Theresa pointed toward the door and Emily nodded, angling across to meet them, still talking ninety miles an hour. As they locked up, Theresa noticed the river's distant murmur carried on the wind. It was a reminder that some echoes demanded to be heard.

Back at the house, she sat on the couch, leaning against Alex while he spoke on the phone with the contractor. She worked from her phone on the blog, the effort of getting the laptop out sounding like too much. She'd already done the hard work on the post earlier, which left just the Publish button to hit on her latest *Kid Quips* blog post, *Whisper Shadows*.

"Hey Quipsters,

Dinner doodles: One witchling sketches a 'whisper shadow' mid-meal—'It guards secrets but lets good ones out!' Family mysteries meet crayon magic.

Your shares light our paths—thank you!

—Miss T"

"Thanks," Alex said, then disconnected the call. "Well, that's that. There's no getting around the extra work. But he said it should have shown up in the prepurchase inspection, so we might be able to push some of the cost onto the corporation we bought it from. Garrett will get that started while he's working on paperwork tonight." Garrett Shea was their main contractor, who also happened to be the electrical contractor. "Sounds like something that happens frequently enough that he's got a process for it."

"That's good news. He seems like a nice guy. What's his background, do you know?"

"Single, volunteers at all the high school football games—not because he has a kid, but because he likes helping." Alex shrugged, turning to the next paper in his pile. "I think he *is* a nice guy."

"Hey, I had a thought about the website."

"What's that? I was just about to email the developer. We can't afford his rates, plus he needs me to act like I know what he'd be doing on the backend. I'm a librarian, not a web developer."

"You know Javi did his recovery at a facility?"

"Yeah." Alex looked at her with a quizzical expression on his face. "What's that got to do with our website?"

"The place where he did his rehab was a technology hub, and he's proficient in dealing with a couple of content frameworks. According to Mia, if we go with a framework, half the work's already done. Plus, that kind of site comes with an admin that sounds a lot like the blog's control panel." She paused and took a breath. "I think we could hire Javi to make the website, and you'll be happier with the process and the result. He's got a list of sites he's worked on before, and another list of sites where he continues to do their updates."

"Sold," Alex said quickly. "He won't talk to me like he's an alien from outer space and I'm just supposed to speak their language. Even if he charges the same, it'll be a mental savings."

"Even better, when I told him what the developer had quoted initially, he gasped. Literally gasped—hand at his throat and everything. Ask him for a quote. He won't make us break the bank to have a good website."

"Have I told you lately how much I adore you, Mrs. Daye-Reed?"

She leaned into him. "Not in the past five minutes, which is a travesty. You should rectify that immediately."

He did.

***

"I made more drawings," Emily announced to the living room, where Theresa and Alex were relaxing on the couch. "I want to play a game, but I'll need both of you."

"You have both of us," Alex told her, his fingers giving Theresa's shoulder a gentle squeeze.

"What kind of game?" Theresa asked, shifting her position on the couch with a slight wince. She scowled playfully when Alex stood and offered her his hand. "Surely I can manage to get myself off the couch."

"You can, but why should you when I'm right here with a perfectly serviceable right hand, ready and willing to assist?" He smiled softly. "Let's make it easy on you for a change."

"Well, when you put it like that…" She held out her hand, gripping tightly as Alex's met her palm. "Heave ho."

"The game, if anyone's still interested, is about a story time, one told only in whispers." Emily stared at Alex for a moment, and he held up one hand. "Yes, sir?"

"Question on point of order."

"Allowed," Emily declared haughtily, causing Theresa to laugh aloud.

"Are voices allowed to whisper too?" He lowered his voice dramatically. "And by that, I mean voices like"—he shifted to chipmunk frequencies—"this, or this, or this." Each "this" came with a comically altered tone, sending Emily into fits of wild laughter at his antics.

"Yes," she gasped, wiping tears from her cheeks. "Daddy A, you can do all of that you want."

"Okay, then I'm ready." He rubbed his hands together eagerly. "Do we have assigned topics or a storyline or what, Em?"

"I made a script drawing for each of us." Emily handed Theresa a sheet of paper covered in careful lines and sketches.

Looking it over, Theresa saw she'd be playing an inn proprietor with a pet parrot. "I think I can really connect with my character. I mean, who wouldn't want a pet parrot?"

Alex glanced at his own paper. "Is this set in stone?"

"What don't you like?" Emily frowned at him.

"It's not that I don't like it, but can you really see me as a pirate with a dog? Why can't I have the parrot?" The corners of his mouth tucked in tightly as he fought back laughter. "I think a dog would be better suited for an inn than aboard a ship on the salty seas. Aargh."

"What's a pirate's favorite letter?" Emily asked, her eyes dancing with mirth.

"I don't know. What is a pirate's favorite letter?" Theresa responded, already knowing the punchline but eager for Emily to deliver it.

"Rrrrrr!" Emily threw herself into an oversized chair, laughing uproariously.

"That's a good one." Theresa grinned. "What does an ocean otter say when they need assistance?"

"I don't know. What does an ocean otter say when they need assistance?"

"Kelp, kelp!"

That had all three of them helpless with laughter, the house echoing back the sounds of joy so warmly that Theresa could almost feel them wrapping around her family, holding them close in their love.

"Okay, no more jokes," Emily said, attempting to straighten her expression. "My character is the daughter of a bookseller, and I have a penguin for a pet. See? We all have ridiculous pets, because it's funnier."

"Fine," Alex said, pretending to be put out.

Their evening continued in that vein as they played Emily's game through to its messy conclusion, The bookseller's daughter stole the pirate's ship, leaving him in need of lodging at the inn. There, the pirate and the innkeeper fell madly in love, while the bookseller's daughter—now turned pirate—sailed off into the sunset, her whispers sounding suspiciously like a ghost.

Theresa and Alex shared a knowing look when Emily refused to be dissuaded from the story as she'd drawn it.

A little later, after Emily had gone to bed, Theresa leaned against Alex's side. "She thought she was subtle about the jealousy, didn't she?"

"She so did. I think she realized it at the end, which is why she started doing my accented voices and making up ridiculous lines for the subordinate pirates. Our Emily has been bitten by the jealousy bug a little bit, I think."

"I believe she has. We'll work through it together. I have faith."

"So do I. Between us, we'll make sure our Em knows she's loved so much."

"And that a new baby doesn't mean less love for her." Theresa turned to face Alex. "Give us a kiss, Mr. Reed. This baby wants me to go to bed early." He bent over and touched his mouth to hers. "Don't stay up too late working on store stuff. I can tell you from having the daycare that the paperwork multiplies every time you acknowledge it exists."

"Is that how that works?" He laughed and stood, then helped Theresa to her feet. "I won't be far behind you."

"Good, I hate sleeping alone."

Chapter 4

The early-evening sun filtered through the garage windows of the Maple Street house, casting dusty beams over boxes labeled in Alex's neat handwriting: "Library Overflow," "Emily's Old Toys," "Family Heirlooms." Theresa and Alex had carved out the afternoon for "baby recon," as Alex called it. They were scouting furniture for the nursery. With the pregnancy now public among close friends—Mia's excited squeals still echoed in Theresa's ears—the nesting urge had hit full force.

Theresa wiped a bead of sweat from her brow, the mild fatigue from morning sickness lingering like a faint whisper. "Okay, Mr. Reed, where's this mythical crib you've been teasing? If it's as legendary as you say, it better not need an exorcism."

Alex chuckled, his eyes sparkling with that sweet enthusiasm she loved. He maneuvered past a stack of old bookshelves, prototypes for Reed Between the Lines, and pulled back a tarp with a flourish. "Behold, the Reed family relic."

There it stood, a sturdy oak crib, its rails worn smooth from generations of little hands. The wood gleamed faintly under the dust, carved with subtle vine patterns along the headboard.

"This was mine, my dad's, and his dad's before him," Alex explained, running a hand over the slats. "Great-grandpa Reed built it by hand in the '40s. It's solid as a storybook ending. There are no drop sides, and it meets all modern standards once we refinish it."

Theresa circled it, envisioning their baby, be they witchling or warlockling, nestled safely inside. The crib had character, history woven into its grains, unlike the sterile models they'd browsed online. "It's beautiful. Sturdy too. Alex, it's perfect for a Reed." She placed her hand on the rail, feeling a soft kick from within her belly, as if the baby agreed. "Got lots of kicks right now. I'd say the little one's voting yes."

Alex's hand joined hers, his face softening with awe. "Our heirloom for the next chapter." But as he inspected closer, his brow furrowed. "Needs work, though. I'll have to sand down the varnish, check the bolts, maybe slap on a fresh coat of nontoxic paint. Nothing a weekend warrior can't handle."

Theresa grinned. "Or a team. Emily can help with the designs. Think she'll want rainbows or protector shadows?"

"Both." Alex pulled her into a hug, the crib standing sentinel behind them. "This feels right, you know? Like we're passing down roots amid all the new whispers."

As they covered it back up, Alex began actively planning a trip to the hardware store, naming off various pieces of hardware.

Theresa's mind drifted to her conversation with Tamika's note. Mysterious whispers and preternatural drawings. But for now, this tangible piece of their future chased the shadows away.

***

Emily sat at the dinner table, methodically eating her salad without even complaining about the croutons, and the crunchiness was something she usually objected to. Halfway through the meal, Theresa felt Alex's foot touch hers, and she glanced up to see him tilting his head toward their girl, eyebrows raised comically high. Emily had stopped eating, her fork tines resting on her plate while she stared into space.

"How was school, Em?"

Emily startled, turning to look at Theresa with wide doe eyes. She blinked fast, then dipped her chin, breaking their gaze.

"Fine."

Oh yeah, that's a lie. Theresa looked over at Alex, whose eyebrows were nearly inching into his hairline now. *He knows it's a lie too.*

"If I'd had a crappy day at the daycare, would you want to hear about it, Alex?" Theresa asked.

His head jolted with two quick nods before his mouth even opened. "Yes, I would. In fact, if you'd had a crappy day and didn't tell me, I might be hurt."

"And if I lied about having a crappy day?"

"Oh, I'd for sure be hurt. We can't share the weight of bad days if we don't share the hows and whys of bad days." Alex raised his voice on the last part, finally catching Emily's attention. "I'd be hurt for sure."

"Why would you be hurt?" It was obvious from Emily's confused expression that she had missed the rest of their little demonstrative conversation.

"If Momma T had a crappy day and didn't tell me. Or worse"—he leaned forward, lowering his voice theatrically—"if she lied about having a crappy day. That'd be the most terrible thing."

"I know you're talking about me." Emily's head dropped, and from what Theresa could see, she looked sheepish. "I didn't mean to lie."

"Then tell us what's going on. We can't help if we don't know." Theresa reached across and captured one of Emily's hands, giving it a squeeze. "I want to help, Em."

"There's a girl in English who's been mean to me. She's never been nice, not even back in the bad days, but now she's really mean."

"How is she mean, Em?" Alex leaned his elbows on the table, resting his chin on his threaded fingers. "What does she do or say?"

"She says my drawings are weird. I was drawing a protector shadow, and she said it was just a bad ghost." Emily's chin lifted. "I'm not the only one she's mean to, though, and I think Sandra is going to tell on her soon."

Sandra was a good friend for Emily—they were the same age and shared similar interests. Sandra had gone to the art camp, too, and that's where their friendship had really been forged.

"If Sandra's going to tell on her, what do you think will happen?"

Emily shrugged. "I don't know. Telling seemed like a baby thing to do."

"Is that what the girl said? That if you told someone, you'd be a baby about it?"

"Yeah, that's it. But I'm not a baby. She just won't leave things alone. It's like if she sees it matters to you, she'll dig a little deeper into it and try to hurt you more." Her voice quavered. Theresa hated seeing her so affected by a bully.

That's the key. We need to call it what it is.

"Then she's a bully. We don't bother with bullies. She's trying to attack you on your art because she knows it means so much to you. Who is it?" She watched Emily's eyes dart back and forth and knew her girl was about to try lying again. "No, don't think of it as being a tattletale. You're sharing the weight of your pain with the two people in the world who love you most. What's her name?"

"Julia."

"Julia Stautter? She's older than you by a year or so, right?" Theresa was pretty sure the girl had been held back due to academic issues.

Emily nodded. "Yeah, she's a little older."

"But she's in your art class?"

"No, she doesn't take art. This is in English. That's the only class Sandra and I have with her."

Older, but in a core academic class with Em.

"Maybe she's angry about something else that's not your fault. Does she pick on other people too?"

"I don't know. Me and Sandra talked about it at lunch the other day. I didn't know she'd been picking on Sandra, too, until we talked."

"Well, I think we've given a bully way too much of our attention today. I do want you to always come to us if you're having problems with anyone. It doesn't matter who it is—we'll always want to know, okay?"

"Yeah." Emily lifted her head, a crooked smile in place. "Maybe she's just mad about something. What if we made apology cookies and I could take her a couple? That might make her happier."

Theresa smiled. "That sounds like a perfect idea, Em. Let's finish supper and clean up, and then we'll check your homework. If everything's in order, I think we've got the ingredients for chocolate chip cookies in the kitchen."

"My favorite!"

***

Monday brought Bonnie's trial day at Sunnybrook Cottage, a buzz of anticipation threading through the usual rhythm. Tamika dropped her off with a nervous hug, whispering to Theresa, "Call if anything unusual happens." Bonnie clutched her sketchbook, her wide eyes taking in the rainbow door like it might be a portal to wonder.

The morning flew past like a breeze. There were exuberant greetings with sticky hugs, followed by art-corner chaos where Emily showed Bonnie how to draw "friendly whispers," which turned out to be swirly lines with smiling faces. But as nap time approached and the glow-in-the-dark stars on the ceiling twinkled like promises, the kids settled onto their mats with soft sighs.

Theresa dimmed the lights, Jasmine's angelic voice lulling them with a gentle song. Mia patrolled the edges, tucking in stray blankets and putting Milo's socks back on.

Bonnie lay quietly at first, but as the room hushed, faint murmurs escaped her lips. The sound was barely audible, like wind through cracks. "The well...whispers cold...fire below..."

Theresa knelt beside her, heart quickening. "Bonnie, sweetie? You okay?"

Bonnie blinked, sitting up with her sketchbook. "The whispering well told me." She flipped to a new page, crayon flying as she sketched out a deep stone well with shadowy figures peering in, flames flickering at the bottom. Water rippled with faint words reading "Help...echo..."

The drawing tied Theresa's stomach in knots. Was Bonnie talking about Shadowbrook's sealed well from last year's mystery? The one with Clara's diary echoes? Bonnie shouldn't know that history. "That's creative, honey. Tell me more?"

But Bonnie just whispered, "It remembers," before curling up again, as if the words had drained her.

Mia sidled over, eyebrow raised. "Kid's got an imagination. Or maybe something else?"

Theresa nodded, taking a quick photo of the drawing for Alex to see. *Whispers from the past, drawing closer.*

As nap time ended, the kids stirred with yawns and quips, lightening the tension-filled air.

Milo stretched dramatically. "Whispers tickle my ears like sneaky fairies! Rawr, fairy chaser!"

Priya giggled. "My whispers are rainbow secrets. I think they color the quiet!"

Janey tugged Theresa's sleeve. "Whispers say...cookie time?"

Landon Hargrove, ever structured, said, "Whispers need a schedule. Should be nap first, talk later."

And Emily, hugging Bonnie, added, "Whisper shadows aren't scary—they're hug echoes!"

The montage of innocence chased the chill away, but Theresa knew the well's whispers demanded answers.

That night, she published a new *Kid Quips* post, titled *Whisper Tickles*.

"Hey Quipsters,

Nap wake-ups: One roars, 'Whispers tickle my ears like sneaky fairies! Rawr, fairy chaser!' Another says, 'My whispers are rainbow secrets—they color the quiet!' Whispers turned whimsical.

—Miss T"

Chapter 5

The reference section of the Willow Creek Public Library felt like a sanctuary amid the growing secrets of the mystery. Alex had spent his lunch break buried in microfiche and old ledgers, his research wizardry in full swing. Theresa joined him after leaving the daycare early again, something Mia had insisted on, citing "owner's pregnancy privileges." Now they pored over yellowed newspaper sheets spread across a wooden table.

"Got something," Alex said, his voice low with excitement. He slid a grainy article from 1923 toward her: "Whitaker Mill Inferno Claims Lives—Survivors Speak of 'Whispering Ghosts.'" The headline jumped out, accompanied by a faded photo of the still-smoldering ruins by the river. "The mill accident left workers trapped in underground tunnels during a flash flood that struck during the fire. Reports say their cries echoed for days, carried on the wind like faint whispers. Locals called them 'echo hauntings' and described them as not something that was supernatural, but rather acoustic anomalies from the river's currents bouncing sounds through the caves."

Theresa leaned in, her hand absently on her belly. "You know, Bonnie's drawings about the fire, and especially the tunnels, are curiouser and curiouser. And her whispers, the things her mom calls 'whisper fits,' they sound just like that, echoed and distant. But how does a six-year-old know this? Tamika said they've barely unpacked."

Alex nodded, flipping to another page. "There's tons of folklore that's built up over the decades. Anecdotal stories of voices on the wind, sometimes even warning of hidden dangers. There are ties to Shadowbrook too. Maybe the estate is connected to those same underground waterways somehow. Maybe Bonnie's picking up on something real. Maybe she's got hypersensitive hearing, or maybe it's inherited echoes? Are we sure they don't have any ties to the town?"

The word *inherited* hung heavy between them.

Theresa's phone buzzed with a text from Tamika. *Can we meet? Found something in family stuff.*

"Speaking of...I just got a text. Tamika wants to talk. Should I suggest Maple Café again?"

Alex gathered the printouts. "I'll come. There's a strength to be had in numbers." He stopped and grinned at her. "And lattes, even decaf ones."

***

Sitting at the café's corner table felt like déjà vu, but this time Bonnie played quietly with crayons at a nearby table, sketching swirls that looked suspiciously like river currents. Tamika appeared more frazzled than before, dark circles under her eyes as she clutched a worn leather-bound book.

"Thanks for coming," she said, sliding what looked to be a diary across. "This was my great-grandma's journal. It was passed down to me years ago, but I never thought of it until I moved back here. I decided to read it when Bonnie's whispers got so much worse. Look."

Theresa opened the fragile pages, yellowed with age. Entries from the 1920s, scrawled in faded ink, descriptions of "whispers from the mill," sketches of flames and tunnels mirroring Bonnie's drawings. One passage was particularly chilling: "The river carries their voices, those of ghosts begging for help. I draw what I hear, though I shouldn't know."

Alex whistled softly. "Your great-grandma worked at the mill? What she wrote down matches the folklore we've uncovered so far. People talking about hearing echo hauntings. Maybe a family sensitivity to sounds, passed down?"

Tamika nodded, tears welling. "She survived the fire but wrote about hearing echoes her whole life. Doctors called it tinnitus or imagination. If Bonnie's inherited it, what do I do? She's been whispering even more, and drawing these every night instead of sleeping." She chuckled, the sound raw and pained. "Which means I'm not sleeping much either. And I'm also not sure of what I'm hearing all the time."

Bonnie looked up then, her voice a faint murmur as she said, "The ghosts say to find the light in the dark." She looked back down and added a crayon flame to her sketch, oblivious to the adults' stares.

Theresa's skin prickled. These weren't just drawings. They felt more like ghostly pleas from the past, whispering through generations.

"We'll do whatever we can to help you and Bonnie find a resolution," Theresa told her. "There's more research to do, and that'll be our next step. In the meantime, don't hesitate to text or call."

"We want to help. Truly we do," Alex offered his support, and Theresa reached out and covered his hand with hers.

"Thank you," Tamika said softly. "That means a lot."

***

The Willow Creek Public Library stood as a sentinel of knowledge, its redbrick facade etched with ivy that whispered secrets to the wind. Gargoyles perched atop the arched entrance like watchful guardians, and inside, the air carried the comforting scents of aged paper and polished wood. Theresa and Alex arrived just after the café meeting with Tamika, the heirloom diary tucked safely in Theresa's tote like a fragile relic. The revelations about inherited echoes had ignited their curiosity, and Alex's librarian instincts were in overdrive.

"Lead the way, research wizard," Theresa teased, looping her arm through his as they stepped into the hushed reference section once again. The high ceilings amplified every footfall, turning their entrance into a soft echo that bounced off the shelves lined with dusty tomes.

Alex grinned, adjusting his glasses with mock seriousness. "Your wish is my command, Mrs. Daye-Reed. But if we find a cursed scroll, you're the one explaining it to Emily."

He steered them toward the microfiche machines in the back, where the town's history slumbered in faded reels and yellowed clippings.

They settled at a long oak table, the kind made shiny by the library's cleaning staff. Alex threaded the first microfiche reel, the machine whirring to life with a mechanical hum. Theresa leaned in as images flickered across the screen—old newspaper headlines from the 1920s, grainy photos of the Whitaker Mill engulfed in flames.

"Look at this," Alex murmured, zooming in on a survivor interview from 1924. "Mrs. Eliza Hargrove—wait, maybe she's related to one of the two branches of the Hargroves we know? She describes hearing 'ghostly pleas' carried on the river winds for months after the fire. Says it drove her brother mad, convinced it was a family curse from their ancestors who built the mill tunnels."

Theresa's eyes widened. "A curse? That sounds like the whispers Tamika mentioned. But tied to a family? What if it's not just acoustics, but maybe something hereditary, like the diary suggests." She flipped through a nearby ledger of oral histories, her fingers tracing entries. "Here's another about a worker named Josiah Pike who claimed the curse stemmed from a lost heirloom, a silver ring engraved with protective runes. It was supposedly stolen during the chaos, and without it, the echoes of the trapped souls couldn't rest. Locals blamed the lost ring for everything from bad harvests to insomnia."

Alex arched an eyebrow, scribbling notes. "A ring? That's new. Could be a decoy, though. Folklore loves shiny objects. But if it's amplifying sounds like the diary implies, maybe it's buried in those tunnels. Or got washed away in the flood and will be nowhere to be found." He paused, glancing at her. "You're glowing, by the way. Pregnancy suits you, even in dim library light."

She swatted his arm playfully. "Flattery will get you everywhere, Mr. Reed. But seriously, this curse angle fits Bonnie's sensitivity. Inherited sensitivity to trauma plus a mythical artifact? Willow Creek's past is like a bad novel, all twisty and full of unresolved plot holes. I swear, this town needs a good editor."

Their banter flowed easily as they delved deeper, a montage of discovery unfolding like turning pages. Alex pulled bound volumes of town council minutes, uncovering several debates about sealing the tunnels post-fire due to "unnatural noises." Theresa cross-referenced those with a folklore compendium, reading aloud snippets about "echo curses" where lost items bound spirits to the living.

"Listen to this. 'The ring was said to hold the mill's secrets, forged from silver mined in the valleys. Lose it, and the whispers multiply, passing through bloodlines like a shadow.' Spooky, huh?"

Alex nodded, his excitement palpable. "It's a classic distraction from the science. But survivor interviews confirm the acoustics are weird down there, even just from the water currents bouncing voices through stone alone. No ghosts, just physics with a folklore twist." He leaned back, stretching. "We should check the genealogy section next. See if Tamika's great-grandma connects to these Pikes or Hargroves."

As they moved to the dimly lit stacks, a sudden flicker caught Theresa's eye. The overhead lights buzzed erratically, casting elongated shadows that danced on the walls. A low hum filled the air, faint and echoing, almost forming words: "Help...dark..."

Theresa froze, her pulse quickening. "Alex? Do you hear that?"

He turned, eyes widening as the lights dimmed further, the hum swelling into a murmur that prickled her skin. "It's just the old wiring. There's probably a storm brewing outside." But even as he spoke, a chill draft swept through, rustling pages on a nearby table like invisible fingers.

Theresa clutched his arm, the minor scare amplifying her pregnancy-heightened senses. For a heartbeat, it felt like the mill's echoes had followed them, the library's silence broken by phantom pleas.

Then, with a pop, the lights stabilized, the hum fading to nothing. Alex exhaled, pulling her close. "Okay, that was creepy. Remind me not to joke about curses." He kissed her forehead. "You okay? Baby okay?"

She nodded, laughing shakily. "Fine. Just our vivid imaginations today. But now I'm starving. These cravings are no joke. I've got a sudden urge for something salty and sweet. Pretzels? Chocolate?"

Alex's eyes lit up with that protective gleam she'd come to adore. "On it. Vending machine raid incoming." He disappeared down the aisle, returning minutes later with a triumphant haul: a bag of pretzels, a chocolate bar, and even a ginger ale for her queasy moments. "Your knight in shining armor, milady. Or at least in librarian khakis."

Theresa beamed, tearing into the snacks as they resettled at the table. "My hero. You know, these little moments? They're what make all this mystery-solving worth it." She shared a pretzel with him, their fingers brushing in a sweet, tender touch. The chocolate melted on her tongue, easing the lingering adrenaline, while Alex's presence wrapped around her like a warm blanket.

Refreshed, they pressed on. After running up against dead ends with more survivor accounts, Alex dialed a number from the ledger. It was of an elderly resident listed as a mill descendant, Mrs. Elara Finch, now in her nineties and living in a nearby retirement home. He put the phone on speaker, the line crackling to life.

"Hello? Who's this?" Mrs. Finch's voice was reedy but sharp, laced with the gravel of age.

"Mrs. Finch? This is Alex Reed from the library, with my wife, Theresa. We're researching the Whitaker Mill fire, and we were hoping you could share some oral history."

A pause, then a chuckle. "The mill? Oh, child, that old ghost story. My grandpappy was a foreman there. Survived the blaze but talked of whispers till his dying day. Said it was the curse of a lost ring that belonged to the Whitaker family, engraved with names of the workers. Or it could have been a watch. I don't rightly remember. He said those folks thought it warded off evil, but after the flood, whatever it was had vanished. Grandpappy swore he heard his lost friends calling through it, like the ring had trapped their voices. Passed the 'gift' down, he did—there are many sensitive ears in our line. But curses? Bah, more like bad luck and bad weather. The river plays tricks, you know."

Theresa leaned in. "Did he ever search for the ring?"

"Tried once, down in them tunnels. Found nothing but echoes and mud. Said the whispers warned him off and to 'leave the dark alone.' But that's just old farmers' tales. Why you asking now?"

"A child's hearing similar things," Alex explained vaguely. "Thank you for your time, Mrs. Finch. This helps more than you know."

Mrs. Finch hummed thoughtfully. "Well, if it's echoes, seal the source. And mind the ring, because if it actually turns up, it might quiet things. Or stir 'em for a much worse outcome. Goodbye now."

They hung up, the call adding layers to the puzzle. Theresa munched another pretzel, her mind whirling. "A ring or a watch? Or a locket? There's a lot of confusion about what the artifact might be. Either way, it's connected to the mill's acoustics."

Alex nodded, packing their notes. "We'll chase it, but carefully. No more scares today."

As they left the library, hand in hand, the setting sun cast long shadows, but the warmth between them chased away the chill of old folklore.

***

Back home, the house hummed with Emily's school project sprawled across the living room. There were family history posters, photos of the Reeds taped alongside Theresa's Daye lineage. But as Theresa helped sort clippings, she noticed Emily's quiet demeanor turned to frowns when the baby was mentioned, and their girl gave them side-eye glances during talk of nursery plans.

"Pregnancy glow suits you, Momma T," Emily said, but her voice lacked its usual spark. "The baby's gonna have everything new, huh?"

Theresa paused, sensing the undercurrent. "New and old. New like the clothing and toys, and old like Alex's crib. What's on your mind, witchling?"

Emily shrugged, focusing on a photo of Alex as a baby. "Just the project."

Later, as Theresa passed Emily's room, she overheard her talking to herself, or perhaps her stuffed unicorn. "The baby's gonna be Reed, like Daddy A. Momma T's Daye-Reed. But I'm still Johnson. Why can't it just go away? Why do I have to be the only one not a Reed? Feels like a bad joke."

Theresa's heart ached. The pregnancy talk had disturbed Emily's peace, something Theresa knew had been hard-won through hours of counseling. It was likely stirring up old wounds from her uncle's abuse. She knocked softly on the doorframe with a tentative knuckle. "Em? Can we chat?"

Emily looked up, pencil pausing. "About the project?"

"About you. Feeling left out?" Theresa sat on the bed, pulling her close. "The baby's new, but you're our first witchling. Totally irreplaceable. And names? They're just words. You're already Reed in our hearts."

Emily sniffled, not meeting Theresa's gaze as she admitted, "But Johnson? It's from before. You know...before the bad stuff."

Theresa hugged her tighter. "We can change that, if you want. When we finalize the adoption papers, we can make your name official too—Emily Reed."

Emily's eyes lit. "Really? Me too?"

"Absolutely. Team Reed, all the way. You and me, and Daddy A, and Baby W."

"Baby W?" Emily was almost bouncing off the bed in her excitement.

"Baby Witchling or Warlockling. You called it, it's gotta be one or the other."

As Emily beamed, immediately turning to draw a new family portrait with all Reeds, those damaging whispers of doubt faded—for now.

That night, as Alex worked on another piece of paperwork for the bookstore, Theresa readied a new *Kid Quips* blog post, *Echoed Secrets*.

"Hey Quipsters,

History hunts: One kiddo murmurs mid-draw, 'The ghosts say find the light in the dark!' Another child says, 'Whispers from the river—sneaky like hide-and-seek!' Past echoes meet like crayon clues.

Your tips help build our bridges—thank you!

—Miss T"

Alex leaned over and kissed her nose, drawing her attention away from the post.

"Let's get some sleep, Momma T. If I'm tired, you've got to be exhausted."

She blew out a breath and nodded. "That I am." Pregnancy fatigue seemed to understand it was being spoken of, because in a moment, she was holding back a jaw-cracking yawn. "Oh." She laughed softly. "Emily wants us to move forward with adoption. She really wants to be a Reed, and I suspect that deadline is before Baby W is born."

"Baby W?"

"Emily asked the same question." Theresa laughed again, leaning her head against Alex's shoulder, letting him lead her to their bedroom. "Baby Witchling or Warlockling. Baby W."

"Makes sense, which makes sense coming from you. You're the most sensible person I know." He folded the covers back on her side of the bed. "Now, go do the things you do in the nighttime that leave you glowing and beautiful. I need a shower. Meet you back here in a few."

"You take such good care of me, Alex. Thank you."

"Don't thank me. Just keep loving me."

"Easiest ask in the world."

Chapter 6

The clang of hammers and the whir of drills filled the air at Reed Between the Lines, transforming the once-quiet storefront into a hive of Saturday activity. It was renovation day, and Alex had rallied the troops. Javi Torres, Mia's brother and Sunnybrook's go-to handyman, had arrived early with his toolkit, ready to tackle the shelving installs and wiring tweaks along with three of his buddies. That would take the brunt of the work from Alex's plate. Theresa tagged along for moral support, though her morning sickness had other plans. It attacked in a queasy wave that had her sipping cool ginger tea from a travel mug.

"Morning, boss man!" Javi called, clapping Alex on the back. His recovery had steadied him into a reliable force, his gambler's past now just a closed chapter. "These shelves? Honey finish is gonna pop. But that tiny roof leak upstairs needs looking at. I talked to the contractor, and we both want to get that fixed before you load up the building with a ton of books. It's been leaking for a while too. There are water stains everywhere."

Alex groaned, running a hand through his hair. "Tell me about it. The contractor said it'd be a quick patch, but delays are stacking up like bad plot twists." He glanced at Theresa, who leaned against a half-built nook, feeling queasier than normal. "You okay, love? Sit. Let me get you a chair."

Theresa waved him off weakly, but another nausea surge had her clutching her mug. "Just the usual unhappy tummy camper. Baby's protesting the drill noise, I think."

Javi chuckled, hauling a ladder over. "My sister was the same with Milo. Even now she says mornings are like wrestling a grumpy koala. Here, let me fix that leak first. Can't have books swimming."

As Javi went into the attic space of the second floor to inspect the roof decking, Alex pampered Theresa with a makeshift throne of stacked cushions and a fresh ginger ale from the mini fridge. "My queen," he said, kissing her forehead. "Rest. We've got this." His eyes softened with concern, mirroring the protectiveness that had deepened since the pregnancy news.

But mishaps mirrored the roof's leaks. Alex stood underneath the opening Javi had crawled through, looking at the drawings the contractor had provided. As he studied the plans, a drip plopped onto them, smudging ink like whispered secrets bleeding through. "Whoa. We've got an active leak!" Javi yelled, scrambling down as a steady trickle followed. Buckets were grabbed, tarps thrown down. There was chaos for a few minutes, water pooling like the river's echoes in Bonnie's whispers.

Theresa took the elevator to the second floor, and she couldn't help but draw the parallel. "Like the mystery. We've got leaks intensifying there too. Tamika texted, said Bonnie's whispers are worse, more frequent."

Alex mopped up, nodding. "And tying to the mill? Those 'echo hauntings' of workers' voices leaking through time. We need to look deeper at that heirloom diary, see what secrets it holds."

"I'd like to talk to her again. I'll message and see if we can come over this evening, maybe return that diary. Not that I think anything paranormal is happening, but I'd rest easier knowing it was out of our house."

"You do that, T. Sounds like a great idea." Alex rested for a moment, wrists crossed over the mop handle. "I want to get things tidied up here before we leave, though. So maybe keep the arrival time a little flexible?"

"Will do." Theresa looked up as Javi came into the room.

"I've got the spot temporarily patched with sealant, but that leak's going to need to be worked on from the roof side of things. I'll get it this afternoon. I've got all the supplies needed for the wiring right here, so I'll work on that next." He adjusted his tool belt. "Growing up, I remember hearing mill rumors about whispers in the wind. If it's leaking history like this roof, better plug it fast."

By midday, the leak had been contained, roof fixed, wiring issues resolved, and there were shelves rising like promises. Theresa felt steadier, likely because Alex's pampering was a balm amid the sawdust. But the mystery lingered, urging them onward.

***

Tamika's modest home on the edge of Willow Creek overlooked the river, its gentle murmur a constant backdrop through open windows. Theresa and Alex arrived that afternoon, the sun slanting low, casting long shadows that danced like faint echoes. Tamika greeted them at the door, looking more exhausted than before. There were heavy bags under her eyes, lips arced into a forced smile.

Theresa handed her the diary, and Tamika took it with a nod. "Thanks for coming," she said, ushering them into a cozy living room cluttered with still-packed boxes and Bonnie's art supplies. "It's getting worse. Bonnie's whispers...I swear they're naming people now. Names from the past."

Bonnie sat cross-legged on the rug, sketchbook open, crayons scattered like fallen leaves. She looked up with those wide eyes, murmuring softly as if to herself or something else. "Elias...trapped in fire...Mary calls from the dark..."

Theresa knelt beside her, heart pounding. "Bonnie? Who's Elias?"

The girl blinked, her voice a faint, echoing whisper as she answered, "He's a mill man. Whispers say he fell, was gone before the water took him." She added to her drawing, a figure in flames, labeled "Elias Jones—no, wait, Whitaker?" The name shifted mid-scribble, as if corrected by an unseen hand.

Theresa felt her face pale. Did she mean Whitaker, like the owners of Shadowbrook?

Alex pulled out his research notes. "Elias Whitaker was one of the mill workers lost in the 1920s fire and flood. Not listed in the survivor accounts. How would she...how would she know that detail?"

Tamika opened the diary and handed it back to Theresa. On the page was written, "Heard Elias's cry in the wind today. Like the ghosts are naming the lost." Her great-grandma's sketches matched Bonnie's, the book filled with images of tunnels, fire, and names etched in margins.

"It's like she's channeling them," Tamika whispered, voice breaking. "The diary mentions a family 'gift' that came as a sensitivity to echoes. But this? It's scaring her. Scaring me too."

Bonnie murmured again, "Mary says to find the locket. It's in the well."

Theresa exchanged a look with Alex. *Shadowbrook's well again*? The revelations were intensifying, history seeping through like the roof's leak.

"We'll help trace it," Theresa promised. "Starting with the old mill site."

As they left, Bonnie's whispers faded behind them, but the names echoed on, each of them demanding to be heard.

That night, Theresa was already in bed working on a new *Kid Quips* blog post titled *Leaky Legends* when Alex got home from the store.

"Hey Quipsters,

Reno quips: One grown-up helper yells, 'Leak like whispers from the past!' Hubby echoes, 'Whispers say…find the cookie in the dark!' Mishaps meet magic.

You're the best!

—Miss T"

She pushed Publish and waited for the success page, then reached over and flipped Alex's covers back.

"I vote you take a quick shower, I'll go make you a quicker sandwich, and then we'll meet back here."

He bent close and kissed her softly, heat rising in her cheeks as it did every time. "Sounds fabulous. I'm beat. Javi's an energy bunny, just go-go-go all day long. I can see where Milo gets it from."

"I'll tell Mia that she can blame her brother for her very own energy bunny." Theresa set the laptop to the side, climbing out of bed. "You know, I'm not that pregnant. It shouldn't be that hard to get back upright. It's like my center of balance is changed."

"From my research on the topic—and yes, of course I've done my research. It's like you don't even know me." He grinned at her, lips quirking to the side. "The out-of-balance feeling can last the whole pregnancy for a small percentage of them. Most often it disappears about the time morning sickness does."

"So there's hope for both things." She made a half-hearted effort to cheer. "Yay."

"Lady, I love you."

"Love you too."

Chapter 7

On Monday night, the playroom at Sunnybrook Cottage Daycare thrummed with an unusual evening energy, having been transformed for their annual parent-teacher night. Low tables held children's portfolios of finger-painted masterpieces, progress reports on kindness-sharing, and notes about snack time. The rainbow rug hosted clusters of chatting parents while the kiddos stayed busy with a giant train set Theresa had set out just before opening.

Theresa circulated with Mia, offering lemon-infused tea and reassurances, but once again the pregnancy fatigue weighed on her like a silent burden.

Whispers, indeed. It seemed that the rumor mill had caught wind of Bonnie's murmurs, twisting them into town gossip.

Mrs. Hargrove cornered Theresa early, her PTA-president aura as sharp as ever. "Theresa, I must say, this 'whispering child' business is concerning. Landon came home talking about ghosts in the nap room! If there's some contagion of imagination running rampant, I expect protocols. His naturopath warns against unchecked fantasies. Says it leads to not only lax morals but also poor academic focus."

Theresa managed to paste on a neutral expression before turning to face the woman. "Mrs. Hargrove, it's just creative play. Bonnie's new, and the kids are bonding over stories. No ghosts, I promise. It's just giggles."

But thanks to Mrs. Hargrove, the rumor spread like wildfire. Mr. Simmon murmured about "echoes from the river," while Mrs. Tennison fretted her twins might "catch the whispers." Mia fielded questions with sarcasm-laced charm, saying things like "If whispers were contagious, we'd all be poets by now." Chaos peaked when Milo demonstrated a whisper by roaring into a parent's ear, "Secret dino attack—rawr!" Laughter diffused some of the tension, but Theresa felt rising stress knotting the muscles in her shoulders. It was like the mystery had found a way to leak into her sanctuary.

Amid the hubbub, Emily pulled Bonnie to the art corner, away from the adult whirl. At ten going on thirty, Emily was a natural mentor, her braid swinging as she spread crayons out. "If whispers are scary, what can we do? We can draw a whisper protector! Remember how? It's like this. We do swirly lines for echoes, but with a big heart to hug them quiet."

Bonnie's eyes lit up, her faint murmurs pausing. "Like shadow friends?" She grabbed a blue crayon, sketching wavy forms with smiling faces. "Mine says they'll protect me from the fire voices."

Emily nodded solemnly. "Yeah! Mine guards the baby. Whispers can't get past hearts."

The girls bonded over their creations, giggles rising as Bonnie's whispers softened to shared secrets. Theresa watched from afar, heart swelling. She felt Emily's kindness was a balm amid the chaos.

As the night wound down, the parents departed with reassurances and leftover cookies, the whispers rumor contained for now.

***

The doctor's office in downtown Willow Creek was a calm contrast to the usual daycare frenzy, its waiting room featuring soft pastel walls and encouraging parenting magazines. Theresa sat beside Alex, her hand in his, the stress of the mystery still simmering just beneath the surface. Bonnie's use of mill-era names like Elias and Mary had kept her up, thoughts echoing through her mind like the river's murmurs.

"Theresa Daye-Reed?" the nurse called. She waited for them next to the hallway before leading the way to the exam room.

Dr. Bernard, warm and efficient, greeted them with a smile. "How's the nausea? And have you had any new symptoms you'd like to talk about?"

"Nausea is mostly manageable with crackers and ginger. Thank goodness it's truly morning sickness. By ten o'clock, I'm generally fine," Theresa said, lying back for the checkup. "I am experiencing more fatigue than I expected, though."

"Fatigue will be unique to each pregnancy. Often it disappears about sixty days after morning sickness, or around the fifth or sixth month."

Alex held her hand as the doctor measured, listened, then prepped the ultrasound.

Dr. Bernard said, "The heartbeat's strong. Would you both want to hear?"

Theresa looked at Alex, and they both nodded at the same time. She squeezed his hand in excitement as the whoosh filled the room, a rhythmic whisper that brought tears to her eyes.

"Our little echo," Alex murmured, blending excitement with the mystery's shadow.

"Everything looks great. Your measurements show the pregnancy is about eighteen weeks along. Have you picked out names yet?" Dr. Bernard asked, printing sonogram photos.

Theresa glanced at Alex. "Discussed, yes. Picked out specific names, not so much. We've talked about picking a name for historical connection. Or maybe something fresh, not usually heard in town. It's hard to know what to name a whole person without knowing even the sex."

Alex squeezed her hand. "We'll decide together. But with the store opening coming up, everything feels a little more stressful than usual. Why don't we set that decision aside until after we know if they're a boy or girl? This little one deserves a peaceful start."

Dr. Bernard nodded sympathetically. "I agree, Theresa. Take your husband's suggestion and remember to take it easy. Next visit, we can check gender if that's still what you want."

Their joint "Yes" was breathy and excited.

As they left, photos in hand, the excitement blended with some residual tension, but joy won the day.

Alex dropped Theresa at home. She'd prearranged with Mia to handle the after-school drop-off and then the parents' pickup time, leaving Theresa to nap in her own bed. She'd learned the hard way that napping in the front seat of her vehicle didn't give much relief to her fatigue.

She woke with a start a couple of hours later, jerked out of sleep by what she was certain was a loud bang. Theresa sat on the side of the bed, listening closely. She didn't hear anything; the house was so quiet it was eerie. A moment later, she thought she heard a whisper that said something like "Did they know?" Goose bumps peppered her arms, a chill skittering down her spine.

Theresa walked through the house, verifying she was there alone. To combat the quiet, she turned on the radio in the kitchen and rifled through supplies in the fridge, sorting out ingredients for an easy Mexican meal: enchiladas, guacamole, and refried beans. She'd have to forgo any really spicy additions, but the idea of the guac made her mouth water.

Alex and Emily came through the door about fifteen minutes later, Emily chattering about school and daycare, Alex coming close for a long, quiet hug. He looked at the stove and laughed. "Supper smells delicious, T. Well done, especially with the threat of an unhappy tummy."

"Maybe guac is my first real pregnancy craving? Pretty healthy, if you ask me. Nothing like the books promise, like pickles and peanut butter."

"If you have an odd midnight craving, it better be available at the gas station, because that's the only store open twenty-four hours." He cradled her belly in both hands, and she leaned back against him, trusting his strength to hold them both. "I can stock up on very firm and very soft avocados for guac if this is going to be the norm. We'll manage either way."

"Why do people even have cravings?" Emily sat on a stool at the breakfast bar. "That's like the sickness. It just doesn't make sense."

"Some people say it's because the baby wants to enjoy a specific food, but I think it's a combination of the memory of scent and taste. Just like the sickness can strike at any time if the pregnant person is exposed to a specific food, like fish." Theresa gagged a little. "See? Just the thought of eating fish has my tummy turning."

"That doesn't make any sense at all. We don't even have fish in the house." Emily rolled her eyes. "Why is it so hard to understand?"

"Because it's something that Momma T and I don't really understand, even though we've both got decades of education," Alex said.

"So me in my fifth-grade classes don't have to know the why. I just have to help Momma T through the when and what."

"That's a perfect way to put it." Theresa gave her little girl a wide grin. "Now, go wash up. The food will be on the table in five minutes." She looked up at Alex. "You, too, mister. You've been working in the store."

He bent close and pressed his lips to hers in a quick kiss. "Yes, ma'am."

Laughing, Emily ran out of the room with a loudly echoed "Yes ma'am."

***

The meeting with their foster coordinator, Ms. Belinsky, and adoption lawyer, Mr. Williams, took place in a bland conference room at the county office, with paperwork stacks mirroring the bookstore's reno blueprints. Theresa and Alex sat across from them, Emily's file open on the table. It included photos they'd submitted of her growth, with regular doctors' reports glowing with progress.

"We've always been on the path to adopt," Theresa said, hand on her belly. "Now, with the baby coming, Emily's asked that we change her name at the same time, if possible, and make her Emily Reed. Make us official before the baby arrives."

Ms. Belinsky smiled. "You've been exemplary parents. Emily's thriving. I have her reports from therapy, and her school marks are stellar. We'll try to fast-track a refresh of the home study."

Mr. Williams nodded, jotting notes. "Johnson ties to her past trauma, and changing to Reed separates that cleanly. If we can find a court date in about two months, would that work? From the looks of things"—he smiled at Theresa—"we've got plenty of time."

Alex leaned forward. "Do you foresee any hurdles? Does the pregnancy change anything?"

"Nope," Mr. Williams assured them. "It strengthens your case, showing you're both stable individuals, expanding your family."

"We may interview people close to you, whether that's family or friends, so don't be concerned if someone mentions it. It's standard," Ms. Belinsky said.

As they wrapped up, Theresa felt a weight lifting from her shoulders, all her mental whispers of doubt about Emily's peace fading. "She'll be thrilled. Team Reed, all in."

Outside, Alex hugged her.

She stood there for a moment, relishing the sense of safety within his arms. "That's one echo resolved. Now for Bonnie's resolution."

***

She returned to the daycare before afternoon snacks, meeting the school bus as it dropped off their after-school kids. She was surrounded by a whirlwind of chattering children including Emily, all talking about their school day, and in Emily's case, an upcoming project for one of her advanced drawing classes.

Theresa ushered the kids inside, waving them to their normal routine of quick snacks, and then the horde of children descended on the art corner. The jockeying for space was a little too quarrelsome for Theresa, and she divided them into three groups, separating their tables and supplies. Emily sat at a table next to Bonnie, and the two girls were thick as thieves, leaning their heads close to chat.

"How'd everything go?" Mia asked.

"Really well. The lawyer thinks we can have court dates within a couple of months. The child services organizer indicated she had all the reports she needed. They might call a few people for interviews about us, and I'd expect them to contact you."

"I'll give them the whole vanilla scoop that is the Reeds' life together." Mia grinned.

"That'd be appreciated," Theresa said with a laugh.

She sat at a table near Bonnie, half-heartedly listening to the kids' conversation while she worked on the computer. Today's *Kid Quips* blog post, *Whisper Protectors*, was about the idea Emily had.

"Hey Quipsters,

Art bonds, because while one kiddo teaches, 'Whisper protectors—swirly lines with hearts to hug them quiet!' another child complains, 'Ghosts in the nap room? My teddy guards better!' Rumors meet rainbows.

Thank you!

—Miss T"

Chapter 8

The scent of fresh sawdust and varnish hung thick in the air in Reed Between the Lines, the bookstore's renovation hitting its peak amid semiorganized chaos. Alex and Javi were working side by side, tearing out a section of outdated paneling on the upstairs wall to make way for what would be a cozy reading loft. Theresa supervised from a safe distance downstairs, her pregnancy making her wary of ladders and dust, though the baby kicked enthusiastically, as if cheering on all the progress.

"Easy does it," Alex cautioned, prying at the wood with a crowbar. The panel gave way with a crack, revealing insulation and something unexpected. "Whoa. Javi, look at this."

Javi peered in, flashlight beam cutting through the gloom. "Old wiring's one thing, but buried treasure? That's new."

Theresa considered the elevator, but it took quite a bit of time to move between the floors. So she climbed the stairs despite her caution, drawn by their excited voices. "What's that? What did you find?"

Tucked behind the panel, still rolled tightly, was a faded parchment-like paper, yellowed with age. Alex unrolled it carefully on the floor to reveal an antique town map of Willow Creek from the 1920s, hand-drawn with intricate details. The river snaked through, the old Whitaker Mill was marked prominently, but what caught Theresa's breath were a series of dotted lines beneath, underground tunnels weaving from the mill to the riverbanks, labeled "Drainage Passages / Echo Chambers."

Alex's eyes gleamed. "A clue. Look at these tunnels. From what I remember of our research, they match pretty closely to the mill folklore. 'Echo hauntings' from water amplifying sounds through hidden waterways. Look at this—there are paths that even connect to Shadowbrook, coming out near where I remember the well to be. If Bonnie's whispers are echoes bouncing from these, they could be coming from anywhere in town. It might explain even the historical names, and for sure the faint voices."

Javi whistled. "Like nature's whisper network. Sounds like your mystery is leaking history through the ground."

The renovations were uncovering literal hidden layers, mirroring the whispers seeping into their lives.

Alex carefully rolled the map back, setting it aside. "We'll show Tamika. This could plug the source."

As they packed up, a loose nail from the wall nicked Alex's hand, a minor mishap that drew attention to the need for a first aid box at the store, even during renovations.

"So much to think of," Alex muttered.

Theresa caught at his arm, pulling him around. "As long as we do it together, it'll never be too much."

Alex huffed out a sigh, then grinned at her. "Love you, Mrs. Daye-Reed."

"Love you back, my favorite guy." She winced. "Now, let's go get you a tetanus booster, because I'm sure you're not up-to-date."

"A shot? It's just a scratch."

"*Are* you up-to-date on your vaccines?"

"How many does a grown man need?"

She sighed. "At least one more, my dear. Come on. I'll get you a sticker if you're good."

***

At home that evening, the house felt like a refuge, a previous dinner's lasagna leftovers reheated amid Emily's school project sprawl. But tension around belonging still simmered, as Emily pushed food around her plate, their conversations absent her usual chatter. The pregnancy talk of nursery colors and baby kicks had dominated lately, and tonight it boiled over.

"Why does the baby get all the new stuff?" Emily burst out, dropping her fork. "New stories, new clothes, new room, new names...I guess I'm just the old one. And the assignment for my whole project is about family history, but it's all Reeds now. All of you, except me!"

Theresa's heart sank, setting down her tea. "Em, sweetie—"

"I'm Johnson! The bad name, from before. The baby's gonna be Reed, perfect. What about me?" Tears spilled over to be dashed away with an angry hand, Emily's jealousy so raw it was painful to hear.

Alex knelt beside her. "You're not sidelined. Not at all. Em, you're the trailblazer. Our first witchling."

Theresa reached out and pulled her into a hug. "And that name? It's going away. It doesn't belong here where we're so happy. Remember, we're changing it. You'll be Emily Reed, official and everything. But you're already family. How would you feel about big-sister duty assignments? We can get a shirt or two made designating you the big sister for everyone to see. We're waiting to pick baby names, but once we know if it's a boy or a girl, we'll need your input on that. I know it feels like a lot of hurry up and wait, but there are some things we can do in the meantime, like design the nursery art. You're the expert on protector shadows, and we all know the baby needs that."

Emily sniffled, then nodded. "Really? I can draw whisper protectors for the crib?"

"Whisper protectors, shadow protectors, maze protectors. You pick, or maybe you do all three. But yes, absolutely," Alex said. "Team Reed needs its captain."

The talk resolved with colored pencils and cocoa, jealousy ebbing like a fading echo with Emily sketching a few options for big-sister shirts, the familial bonds strengthened as they came out the other side.

***

Alex came home the next day from the library, his face alight with purpose despite renovation dust on his jeans. He found Theresa in the sunroom, blogging quips, and dropped a kiss on her head. "Great news. I took the map over to the library to consult with the archivist. She confirmed it's authentic and that there are tunnels underneath the mill."

Theresa tilted her chin to silently ask for a kiss and received a quick buss on the lips. "That's fabulous news. Great idea about securing expert prowess."

"Yeah, that's great. Oh, I want to tell Celia about the baby. Little Lily will be thrilled for a new cousin. I've been a little worried they'd find out from chatty kiddos."

Theresa smiled. "Of course. Should we do a video call?"

"Sounds good. Hey, we might as well loop in my parents too. Right now they're vacationing in Florida, probably golfing." He paced, all his excitement mixed with an uncommon case of nerves. "Mom will cry, and Dad'll joke about spoiling grandkids. Can we do it now?"

"Get Em. She's important to these discussions."

He nodded. "Right. Be back."

Theresa set up the laptop in the living room, Alex and Emily joining. Emily held one of the big-sister drawings, and Theresa knew all the Reeds would pick up on that clue quickly. The call connected, and they saw Celia beaming from her screen, his parents tanned and waving from a sunny patio on theirs.

"Family meeting?" his mom teased.

Alex grinned. "Big news. We wanted to tell everybody—"

"I think I know," his sister interjected, and Alex scowled at the screen. "Shushing now," she said, pretending to lock her lips.

"So, as I was saying before I was so rudely interrupted, we're expecting! Baby Reed, due in five months."

Screams of joy erupted, with his sister high-fiving the camera and his mom predictably tearing up. "Another grandbaby! Lily will be over the moon."

His dad chuckled. "Boy or girl? Need to stock the fishing gear."

Emily piped up, "Witchling or warlockling! And I'm big sis—look!" She held her drawing higher to a chorus of "oohs" and "aahs."

The call bubbled with questions about names and nurseries. Alex's father was brought to tears at the news that they would be using the family crib.

As they signed off, Alex hugged Theresa. "Our circle grows. Mysteries can't touch how this feels."

That night, Theresa's *Kid Quips* blog post was about *Big Sis Whispers*. She wrote about the resolution of jealousy changing the feeling to love instead.

"Hey Quipsters,

Family flares, while one witchling declares, 'Baby gets new stuff—I'm the old one!' Resolved with 'You're the expert on protector shadows—baby needs that too!' Jealousy to love.

Your confidence in us strengthens our bonds—thank you!

—Miss T"

Chapter 9

The afternoon hush at Sunnybrook Cottage Daycare carried an unusual weight, the kind that prickled the skin like static before a storm. Nap time had wrapped up, kids stirring with yawns and stretches under the glow-in-the-dark stars, but Theresa lingered in the playroom, tidying mats with a distracted air. The mystery's suspense had built steadily because Bonnie's whisper fits were intensifying, her drawings now naming more mill victims, like "Mary the weaver." It felt like the mystery had seeped into every quiet corner of Theresa's mind.

As she stacked pillows in the reading nook, a faint murmur drifted from the vents—soft, echoing words, indistinct but insistent. "Hel...dark...fi..." Theresa froze, her hand on her belly, the baby's kick a sharp reminder of vulnerability.

Whispers at the daycare? Her pulse raced. Was this Bonnie's echo haunting spreading out to new locations or something more sinister?

"Mia!" she called softly, not wanting to alarm the children.

Mia poked her head in from the kitchenette.

"Come here a sec." She waited for Mia to approach. "Do you hear anything odd coming from there?" Theresa pointed to the vent. The murmurs continued, faint as wind through reeds.

Mia's eyes widened. "Creeping creepy creeps. It sounds a lot like Bonnie's thing."

They listened together, the words looping: "Col…echo…"

Theresa's mind flashed to the mill tunnels, the river's acoustic tricks. But when Mia grabbed a step stool and peered into the grate, she snorted. "Red herring alert. Up here, I don't hear anything other than the wind whistling in through the old vents. Must be a draft from that loose panel Javi fixed last week, amplified by the river breeze outside."

Theresa exhaled, relief mingling with lingering unease. "Wind in vents. That makes all the sense. But with the mystery and everything, it just felt too real."

Mia hopped down. "Pregnancy hormones amping the suspense? Or maybe Willow Creek's just that whispery. Either way, I'll get Javi to seal it from the outside. I'll close the vent for now. Can't have ghost sounds scaring the kiddos."

As they closed the grate temporarily, the whispers faded to a harmless hum. But the event left Theresa on edge, because echoes or not, the past seemed to be murmuring louder.

Later, a gruff Officer Daniels stopped by unannounced, his unexpected visit buffered somewhat by a box of donuts he brought for the staff. "I heard about the Sullivan kid's issues. It's just town talk generated by some ventriloquist trick. I wouldn't worry about it if I were you. Her mom, Tamika, seems to fit in here in Willow Creek well."

Theresa poured him coffee in the kitchenette. "Have you been hearing negative comments?"

"Just from Mrs. Hargrove, but when isn't she complaining about something? I know from the chatter that Ms. Sullivan has family ties to Willow Creek, so it makes sense that she'd relocate here. I guess her great-grandma was a mill survivor, noted for hearing voices after the fire. Doctors back then called it hysteria. Now they'd label it maybe PTSD or a sensory thing. Long ago, it could be called a possible family curse, but probably sensitive hearing amplified by stress. All kinds of stuff skips a generation. My mom had red hair, but you had to go back to her great-grandparents to find out where it came from. That little kid's drawings? They're just echoing that old pain."

Theresa nodded, piecing it together with Alex's research. "Like a generational echo. Thanks, Officer Daniels. I'm all for any information that keeps us from chasing ghosts."

He grunted. "Real or not, watch your back. Whispers have a way of stirring up trouble."

As Daniels left, the suspense in her gut coiled tighter. Was the so-called curse a decoy or the key to Bonnie's murmurs?

***

Work balance teetered that afternoon when chaos erupted in the art corner, a glitter explosion of epic proportions, courtesy of Milo's "whisper game" turning into a sparkle ambush. Glue bottles toppled, jars overturned, and there was rainbow mayhem everywhere.

Mia dove in like a superhero, her sarcasm a shield. "All right, sparkle squad, we're playing the Freeze Game! So freeze. Stay still while I see what can be salvaged." She corralled the giggling culprits, handing out wet wipes while Jasmine sang a cleanup tune to keep spirits high. "I've got this, Theresa. Go blog. Pregnancy pass activated. Kids, this is your first reminder that Milo's dino roar did not mean 'dump the glitter bin!'"

Grateful, Theresa retreated to the kitchenette, laptop open. The glitter fiasco sparked the inspiration for a *Kid Quips* post on "whisper games" to lighten the mystery's shadow.

She drafted quickly, smiling at the kids' antics filtering through the door as she wrote a post titled *Whisper Games.*

"Hey Quipsters,

Glitter gone wild. One kiddo declares, 'Whisper games need sparkles for fairy secrets!' Another, 'My whisper exploded like a rainbow dino. Rawr!' Games turned glittery. We're sorry in advance for the state of your washing machine.

Your responses sparkle our days—thank you!

—Miss T"

As she hit Publish, Mia poked her head in, the shine of glitter still in her hair. "Crisis averted. I told everybody that next time, the whisper games stay verbal. No props!"

Theresa laughed, the balance between chaos and control in the cottage restored for the moment.

***

Alex worked late into the night at their kitchen table, the glow of his laptop casting shadows across printouts of order forms and supplier catalogs. The deadline for the first really big book order for Reed Between the Lines loomed, and he was deciding between romances, mysteries, cozies, thrillers, and kids' books to stock the shelves.

As midnight neared, Theresa stirred in bed, the bane of every pregnant woman calling. Just another bathroom trip. Padding down the hall in slippers, she noticed the light on in the kitchen and found him dozing in his chair, cheek propped on a catalog, soft snores whispering like the mystery's echoes.

She smiled tenderly, shaking his shoulder. "Hey, book wizard, it's past your bedtime. The order can wait."

Alex blinked awake, rubbing his eyes. "Just finalizing…some stuff. I think the publisher's deal is gold, but quantities could be a make-or-break for us."

"Tomorrow," she insisted, pulling him up. "Tomorrow is soon enough. Emily needs a rested dad. So does the little one, and me."

He hugged her, hand on her belly. "Our little echo agrees. Let's go to bed, my love."

They shuffled to bed, where the whispers of work and worry faded to quiet dreams and sweet slumber.

Chapter 10

The old Whitaker Mill site loomed on Willow Creek's outskirts, its crumbling skeleton overgrown with ivy and shadowed by the river's bend. Theresa and Alex had been inside it more than once, back during their first partnership for a mystery that gained them a marriage and a daughter. So for them, the building held fond memories.

The two of them and Tamika Sullivan had agreed on a group exploration, meaning a cautious daytime trek to chase the whispers' source. They came armed with flashlights, Bonnie's latest drawing, and as the current owner of the property, they had Claire Pike's reluctant blessing as long as they promised no heroics, and to call the authorities if it got "weird"—Claire's word.

Tamika carried Bonnie through the undergrowth, the little girl's sketchbook peeking from her backpack.

The air hummed with the river's murmur as they picked through weeds, the mill's remnants evoking faded photos from Alex's research. "We could go into the basement, but from what I've read, the tunnels should begin near the outside edge of the foundation," he said, consulting a copy of the antique map from the bookstore walls. "They're drainage passages, which would be perfect for acoustic echoes."

Tamika nodded, tense. She held Bonnie's head against her shoulder, blocking her ear. "Last night, Bonnie drew a dark hole with whispers pouring out. Said 'the entrance calls.'"

Behind a rusted grate, half buried under silt, was a narrow tunnel entrance, the stone walls slick with moisture and the faint drip of water echoing inside. Bonnie's drawing matched eerily to the jagged opening, her swirling crayon lines for "whisper winds."

"Look," Theresa murmured, shining her light in. The beam revealed graffiti-scrawled walls and a low ceiling, but as they listened, faint voices seemed to carry on the draft: "Hel...cold...fi..." Audibly echoing, sounds distorted by the river's flow through hidden waterways, but it was an acoustic anomaly, not ghosts.

Tamika gasped. "That's what Bonnie hears. How do the echoes form? The mill accident?"

Alex knelt, map in hand. "No, I don't believe so. The flowing water is amplifying the sounds. These aren't old cries trapped in the currents, bouncing forever. It's the combination of the rushing water and the formation of the tunnels and vents, paired with Bonnie's sensitivity that picks them up like a radio."

Bonnie tugged Tamika's sleeve, whispering, "Momma, they say 'find us.'"

The group shared a chill, but the past's pleas had already been revealed as tragic science, not of supernatural origins. But the tunnel's depth hinted at more. Perhaps there were artifacts amplifying the anomaly.

They emerged from the underbrush, Alex using rocks to temporarily seal the grate. "We need experts in this field to seal it properly," he said. "See if we can't end the 'hauntings' for good."

"I know if we approach Claire with this, she'll have an expert on hand before you can say 'boo,'" Theresa replied.

Tamika hugged Bonnie tight. "Thank you. Her whispers, they might finally fall quiet."

As they left, the river's murmur followed them, a reminder that some echoes demanded closure.

***

That evening, after picking Emily up from Mia's, where she'd been creating a block pyramid with Milo, and amid the cozy clutter of the living room with Emily's family history project still taped to the walls, a question came unexpectedly out of left field. Emily sat cross-legged on the floor, coloring on the coffee table, making a whisper protector for Bonnie, but her pencil paused.

"Momma T? When am I gonna become a Reed? Like, for real? Do we know when I get to talk to the people about what I want?"

Theresa looked up from her decaf tea, Alex pausing mid-bite of a chocolate pie he'd brought home from the local bakery. "What brought that on, witchling?"

Emily shrugged, eyes down. "The project's got all the Reeds, Daddy A. But I'm still Johnson on paper. When does it change? Before the baby?"

Alex set his fork down. "Soon, Em. We told you we've met with the lawyer and coordinator, and they're confident it will happen quickly. A court date in weeks. You'll be Emily Reed officially."

Theresa reached for her hand. "And in our hearts? You already are."

Emily beamed, resuming her drawing, saying quietly, "Good. That's good. Cuz Johnson whispers bad stuff. Reed's better, like protectors."

The moment warmed them, with the promise of paperwork helping solidify their found family ties.

***

The next day, a pregnancy checkup loomed, a routine appointment to check progress. Theresa waited in the exam room for several extra minutes, hand on her belly feeling the soft thumps of kicks. Her texts went unanswered, and the stress was busily turning her stomach as badly as morning sickness. As minutes ticked by, it was obvious Alex was going to miss the appointment.

Dr. Bernard proceeded kindly. "Baby's thriving, Theresa. A nice strong heartbeat. Let's come back in a week for the sonogram. I'll make sure the receptionist sets the appointment." Her words and care were kind, but seeing the empty chair still stung.

Alex burst in just as the visit wrapped up, breathless. "I'm so sorry. The contractor at the bookstore found something in the loft beams. Couldn't leave 'til it was squared away. Safety first."

Theresa stayed quiet until they were waiting on the appointment card from the receptionist. She looked at him and nodded, hurt lingering despite the good excuse. "I get it. But a quick text would have told me you were running late. You didn't even respond to my questions, Alex. I needed you here."

He pulled her into a hug outside. "I know. I won't let it happen again. Team Reed comes first. We've got our priorities straight."

The sting faded slowly, the bookstore's demands echoing the mystery's pull, where balance might always be a delicate dance.

****

Midnight cravings struck like a lightning bolt in the dark. She woke wanting chocolate and pretzels, a delicious-sounding combo that had Theresa giggling as she nudged Alex awake. "Baby's demanding a snack run. We don't have anything I want here. But maybe if you went to the bookstore, you could raid the contractor's snack stash?"

Alex rubbed his eyes, grinning. "Midnight mission? I'm on board. Let's go."

Theresa shook her head. "I'll stay here in case Em wakes, but what you're looking for is savory and sweets mixed, more specifically chocolate and pretzels. If you can find them."

Alex dressed and left, and Theresa leaned back in the bed, feeling fatigue creeping in around the edges. She rubbed her baby bump with one palm. "You're already making your wants and needs known, little one. I can't wait until you're here with us."

She heard the garage door going down and sat up, realizing she'd dozed off while leaning against their pillows. Alex came in, having retrieved the necessary snacks, and proceeded to pamper her with a makeshift picnic on the bed. "Cravings conquered. Is the baby happy? How about the baby's momma?"

She leaned into him, the funny snack run blending fatigue with joy. "We all are."

Alex ate his share and then lay back, looking up at Theresa with a warm expression on his face, lips curled in a slight smile. He blinked, and she looked away for a moment to set her lemon-lime soda on the nightstand. When she turned back, he'd fallen asleep.

It took Theresa a couple of hours to get back to sleep, so she used the time productively, working on the laptop to set up the next *Kid Quips* blog post, *Whisper Calls*.

"Hey Quipsters,

We've had some recent exploration echoes. One kiddo says, 'The entrance calls like a secret game!' Another vows, 'Whispers from the dark? My flashlight wins!' Adventures multiply like wonders of the world.

Your tips light our tunnels—thank you!

—Miss T"

Chapter 11

The soft hum of Dr. Macy's office provided neutral ground for the emotional unraveling, its walls adorned with calming abstracts and shelves of children's books on feelings. Theresa had arranged the session, tying Bonnie's whispers to therapy, much like Emily's maze drawings and Leon's shadows had needed. Tamika Sullivan sat rigidly on the couch, Bonnie playing quietly with blocks in the corner, while Theresa and Alex observed supportively from side chairs, invited by Tamika to stay when they would have gone to the waiting room.

Dr. Macy, warm and professional, leaned forward. "Tamika, you've shared Bonnie's whispers and drawings. They sound distressing, something like faint echoes that mirror possible historical scenes. Let's explore what might be underneath."

Tamika fidgeted with the heirloom diary in her lap, her voice cracking. "It's not just her. I think I hear them, too, sometimes. Faint, like the wind. I always thought it was just my imagination, but in the diary, my great-grandma wrote that she heard the same. She survived the mill fire, but her brother—he died in the tunnels. Drowned in the flood. My mom called it a 'family whisper,' like a sensitivity to sounds, amplified by trauma. Said it was passed down like a curse."

The room stilled, the emotional core laid bare. Theresa's hand tightened on Alex's at the thought of inherited trauma echoing through generations like the river's anomalies.

Dr. Macy nodded gently. "Not a curse. It's likely something along the line of hyperacusis or auditory processing disorder, which has been found to be hereditary in some families. The mill's echoes could trigger it, especially if you're near the river. Bonnie's whispers? They're her way of processing overwhelming input. Tell me, as a baby, did Bonnie ever react to sounds differently than you would have expected?"

"Yes. I needed to make sure she was asleep with the door closed before I could wash dishes or she would scream like nothing I'd ever imagined a baby could. There were other things, like going through a car wash would set her off. I just learned how to avoid those triggering sounds." Tamika leaned forward. "That hyperacusis, does it work like that?"

"Exactly like that. I'm going to refer you to an audiologist I've worked with before. They'll define the parameters of the sound 'triggers,' as you called them. Then, with that information in hand, we can follow up with occupational and speech therapy. And of course my door will always be open." Dr. Macy put a hand over Tamika's trembling one. "Therapy can help, sometimes for the whole family. We'd lean into mindfulness for both of you, and sound desensitization. Like I've done with other clients, helping them turn fears into tools."

Bonnie looked up, whispering faintly, "Brother in the dark…whispers say goodbye."

Tamika's tears fell. "Great-grandma's brother—Elias. She never forgave herself for surviving. If it's trauma echoing…maybe I can break it for Bonnie."

Dr. Macy smiled. "You already are just by seeking help. Sessions together, perhaps? Rewrite the whispers into stories of strength."

As they scheduled follow-ups, relief washed over Theresa. This was another family's secret confessed, the core of decades of emotional weight lifting like mist burning off the river.

***

At home that evening, the house buzzed with Emily's latest invention, a "whisper hunt" game, born from Bonnie's descriptions and Em's school project curiosity. The living room became a makeshift maze of blankets and pillows, flashlights casting playful shadows.

"Okay, rules!" Emily declared, unicorn notebook in hand. "Hide and whisper clues—like secrets from history. Find 'em with protectors!"

Theresa and Alex joined, crawling under forts as Emily hid paper "whispers" with facts from her project. "The river whispers old mill stories!" But as the game unfolded, it turned educational, with Emily pausing to explain. "Whispers aren't scary. They're probably just echoes, like Bonnie's. She said Dr. Macy said we can hug them quiet."

Alex whispered a clue. "Family history hides in tunnels. We need to find the map!"

Emily giggled, uncovering it. "Like our Reed history? No bad whispers there."

Theresa pulled her close mid-hunt. "Exactly, witchling. Games like this teach us to listen, and to heal."

The hunt ended with cuddles all around, their whispers turning to full-blown laughter at Alex's different voices, the entire evening proving an educational balm for the mystery's murmurs.

***

Mia's voice cut through the daycare's morning prep the next day, her tone playful amid the cubby chaos. "Okay, team. You've gotta have my back. Spill all about dating after kids. I'm thinking of dipping a toe back in. Javi's stable, Milo's in school, so who's got hot tips for me?"

Milo, stacking blocks nearby, froze. "Date? Rawr!" He refused to elaborate, only roaring in response to his mother's questions, his dino shield firmly up.

Jasmine laughed, her angelic voice light. "My sister jumped in after her kid started school. She started chatting on the dating apps, and a couple of those led to coffee meetups. She said it was a lot like glitter—part messy, but also part sparkly. She finally found a keeper who loves kid chaos."

Sarah, their quiet assistant, blushed while sorting markers. "I've never dated. Too busy with my degree, then here. Dating." She shivered. "That's a scary thought."

Mia grinned, a glitter pencil holding her messy bun in place. "We'll workshop it. Theresa? Pregnancy glow got any romance advice?"

Theresa smiled. "Date nights with books, which was Alex's specialty. But go slow, Mia. You've earned sparkles."

As Milo rawred again, the talk lightened the air amid the daycare's steady rhythm.

That night, Theresa's *Kid Quips* blog post was titled *Whisper Hunts* for Emily's game.

"Hey Quipsters,

We had some game giggles, where one witchling whispers, 'History hides in tunnels. Can you find the map?' Another rawrs, 'Whispers say—dino attack!' We've found that hunts turn history fun.

—Miss T"

Chapter 12

The soft opening of Reed Between the Lines buzzed with Willow Creek's small-town warmth, the bookstore's doors propped wide like an invitation to adventure. String lights twinkled overhead, mirroring the daycare's anniversary setup. Tables groaned with local treats, from Sweet Rise Bakery cookies to Maple Café lattes, and there were stacks and stacks of books ready for browsing.

Alex had tried to keep it intimate, inviting just their friends, his old library staff, and some of the daycare's parents, but the rumor mill had spread the news far and wide like river mist, adding an unexpected buzz that came from the excitement of a new business opening.

Alex greeted guests with his affable charm, Theresa by his side, her sundress hiding the gentle swell of her belly. "Welcome to our literary lair!" he called, as Officer Daniels grunted approval over a mystery novel.

Emily darted around, handing out "whisper protector" stickers she'd drawn, which was her way of weaving the mystery into the fun.

Theresa overheard a few folks chatting about the recent town talk about old echoes, verbally tying them to the mill's old folklore, and turning portions of the opening into an impromptu storytelling hub.

The rumor about the whispers brought an unexpected intensity to the event. Clusters of parents stood chatting, sharing tales. Then an elderly guest, Mr. McCowel, the foster coordinator's father, sidled up after Alex's welcome speech. "Got yourself a fine shop here, son. Kinda reminds me of the old mill days, back when my pa worked there. Was a fine place to work too. Never heard about whispers until the fire, and the flood. We never thought it was ghosts. Old rumors have them being echoes from a hidden artifact. It might have been a foreman's locket, lost in the tunnels. Inscribed with names of the lost, said to amplify cries like a megaphone."

Theresa's ears perked up at the clue. The story of the locket matched some of Bonnie's drawings, pointing to the mill's underground. She asked, "Mr. McCowel, any idea where?"

He shrugged. "Riverbed, maybe?" He sounded tired. "Washed away in the flood, like so many things."

Mia arrived with Milo in tow, Javi trailing with a toolbox brought along just in case. Mia said, "The place looks epic, Alex. All your hard work coming to fruition, that's gotta feel good."

He looked around, seemingly in awe. "Yeah, it really does."

The event hummed on, books flying off shelves, Alex's brand-new payment system getting all the bugs worked out of it as sales flowed.

As closing neared, he hugged Theresa. "I'd count this soft opening a rousing success, in spite of the ghostly PR."

She smiled. "Maybe because of it. And we have a clue. The artifact, that's our next step."

***

The ultrasound appointment the next morning felt like a milestone wrapped in anxious anticipation, the doctor's office a quiet prelude to family growth. Theresa lay back, gel cool on her skin, Alex holding her hand tightly with Emily on his lap—he'd made sure none of them would be missing this appointment. Dr. Bernard's tech moved the wand slowly, angling it this way and that, the screen flickering to life with their baby's form. They saw tiny limbs waving, the heart thumping strong.

"Everything's perfect and measuring a definite twenty weeks. Want to know the gender?" Dr. Bernard asked from her position behind the tech.

Theresa glanced at Alex, who nodded. He gave Emily a squeeze, and she all but shouted, "Yes! Oh yes, please tell us."

"It's a girl," the doctor announced, printing photos. "Healthy and active."

"A witchling," Emily crowed as Theresa's eyes misted, Alex's grin a mile wide.

"Witchling two," he whispered, kissing Theresa's hand.

"Meet your little sister," Theresa said.

Emily's eyes widened, fingertip reaching out as if to trace the image. "Really? A witchling? Like me?" She hugged them both fiercely. "I can teach her protectors, and that whispers aren't scary!"

The reveal strengthened their family's bonds. Emily's big-sister role was solidifying, with family echoes harmonizing amid the day's murmurs.

***

The lawyer's office was a stark contrast to the bookstore's warmth, its conference table piled with paperwork for Emily's adoption and name change. Mr. Williams greeted them efficiently, Ms. Belinsky nodding approval from her seat.

"We'll be finalizing everything before the judge," Mr. Williams said, sliding forms toward them. "The home study has been updated, with glowing reports. I have Emily's consent form. And I heard from the interviewer that she's excited?"

Theresa smiled. "Beyond. Wants to be a Reed before the baby comes."

Alex signed the paperwork with steady hands. "This will make us whole."

Mr. Williams reviewed their next steps. "Court next week should be totally routine. From where I sit, the judge'll approve. He'll let me know ahead of time if he sees something to throw up a roadblock, but I don't expect that to happen. From all metrics, your family's exemplary."

Ms. Belinsky added, "Emily's thrived with you. This seals it."

As they left, papers in hand, Theresa felt another weight lift, this time of legal echoes resolved, paving the way for far brighter future paths.

***

Mia had a potential coffee date to get ready for, so Theresa had gone to the cottage to manage the pickup rush. A storm was brewing, so afterward, Theresa and Emily drove by the bookstore to pick up Alex so he wouldn't have to walk home in the rain.

Finally, the three of them were all safely home, thunder rolling outside. Theresa was sitting on the couch, unwinding after another busy day, when a series of thumps came from the side door that opened into the kitchen. Alex approached it carefully and peered through the window before opening the door wide.

Theresa's phone rang, Mia's contact info on the screen.

"Milo, what are you doing out this time of night?" Alex said, scooping a very wet Milo into his arms.

"Theresa, I can't find Milo!" Mia screeched from the speaker on her phone. "He's gone."

"He just showed up here. Just as you called," Theresa told her.

"Is that Mommy?" Milo started twisting in Alex's arms, shouting, "Rawr, rawr, rawr, Mommy."

"Oh my God, he's there? He's okay?" The sound of the call changed, and Mia told someone, "He's at my boss's house. I need to go right now. Sorry." The sound changed again, and she heard Mia transition outside. "I'm about five minutes away. Three of that will be hobbling in high heels to my car."

"Just take them off."

"Jesus, why didn't I think of that? Oh, Javi's calling. He's the one who discovered Milo was missing. I need to get this."

"We'll see you when you get here."

"Mommy, rawr," Milo said before Theresa hung up.

Emily ran down the stairs. "Is that Milo I hear rawring? What's rawring wrong?"

Alex looked clueless, and Theresa reached out for the little boy, pulling him onto her shrinking lap. He leaned against her shoulder, frame starting to shake with sobs and the cold.

"Get a blanket, Em, would you?" She looked up at Alex. "Mia's on her way. Can you find him a shirt to trade out for his wet one?" Both of her helpers scurried away on the tasks set for them, and Theresa turned to Milo. "You're pretty upset, huh?"

"Rawr," he said, at only a fraction of the volume he'd used before.

"It's scary to make changes in our lives. Like Emily was afraid of the baby taking her place. Mr. Alex and I know that making a family bigger doesn't give everyone a smaller share of love; it gives everyone more love, because there's more people to love. Your mommy isn't nearly at the same place Mr. Alex and I are, so you've got a long time coming with her love all to yourself. But her adding someone isn't bad. Remember before your Tio Javi came to live with you? Did you have more love back then?"

"Rawr." He shook his head.

"Nope, you had more love when Tio came to live with you. See? More people equals more love." Theresa pulled him tight against her, whispering in his ear, "But she'll never love anyone even half as much as she loves you."

Alex beat Emily back by only a step or two, both laughing at having turned it into a harmless competition. By the time they had Milo situated with an outgrown shirt of Emily's and wrapped in a cozy blanket, Mia's headlights shone through the windows.

Alex opened the door just in time for her to come running inside, eyes only for Milo. She swept him up out of Theresa's lap, cuddling him close as she whispered to him, "You scared me, half-pint. Scared Tio too. I'm so glad you're okay." She kissed one cheek and then the other, then gently pulled one ear. "I'm ditching the idea of dating for a while, so hopefully we won't see a repeat of this little excursion."

Milo shook his head. "No."

"No? No, you don't want me to date? I think I got that message loud and clear, boyo."

"No, you can date. I want more love." He nodded, tucked his head along his mother's neck, and promptly fell asleep.

"I don't understand," Mia said quietly. "He didn't even rawr at me. Not once."

"I'll tell you everything tomorrow," Theresa replied. "Why don't you get him home now and in bed. I hate he did it, but I'm glad Milo felt like he could come here when he was upset."

"You were the only person I could think to call."

"And I hate you had to, but I'm glad you did."

Alex reentered the room with an umbrella. "Let me keep you guys dry while you put him in his car seat." He ushered them out, leaving Emily staring at Theresa.

"He was mad?" she asked.

"He was jealous. Of something that hadn't even happened yet. It's hard to explain your feelings when all you feel like you can do is rawr." Theresa stifled a yawn.

"Big sister, I'm going to head up to bed. Tell Daddy A for me?"

"He was jealous? Like me with the baby, way back when I didn't understand?"

"Yes, witchling, way back then, a couple of weeks ago." She grinned and opened her arms. "I need a witchling one hug, please, ma'am."

Emily engulfed her with a hug, pressing a quick kiss to the baby bump. "Night, witchling two."

As Theresa prepared for bed, she ran Emily's reasoning through her head again. When Alex came in, she said, "We're really lucky that Emily understood so quickly that the baby was a good thing. I can't imagine if she'd run away. I'd have been so sick with worry."

"Me too," he agreed, setting a preemptive packet of crackers and an opened lemon-lime soda on her nightstand.

Theresa ducked her head, hiding her grin. "Love you, Mr. Reed."

Sweeping her up in his arms, he walked to her side of the bed and slowly dropped her until her toes reached the floor. "And I love you."

Chapter 13

"I'd like to go back into the tunnels," Alex announced as they prepared for their day. "I think there's something to be learned from how the wind and the sound of the water join to make the whispers that Tamika and Bonnie both hear."

"I don't want you going down there alone," Theresa told him. "I'll come with you. We've got the map and have limited chances of getting lost."

"I don't want you down in the tunnels." He wrapped an arm around her from behind, hand cradling her belly tenderly. "Seems like a bad idea."

"Then it's a bad idea for my baby daddy too." Theresa straightened, turning in Alex's hold and staring him in the face. "I vote we go together or we don't go at all. Team Reed."

"T, I just...This seems like a non-pregnancy thing to do."

"Team Reed."

His eyes closed, and she could nearly see him counting to ten. "Let me think about it."

"You promise me right now that you will not go into the tunnels or even back to the old mill without me." Theresa caught his slight flinch and laughed. "You act like I don't know you, mister."

"Okay, I promise." He cupped her face in his hands, pressing a sweet kiss to her lips. "I'll see who we can bring along for backup."

"As long as it includes me." Theresa leaned her forehead against his chest, relaxing.

***

They'd returned to the site at midmorning, a photocopy of the antique map from the bookstore walls once again clutched in Alex's hand like a talisman.

Officer Daniels had been next in line for a coffee and had overheard Alex talking to Claire Pike. He'd insisted on tagging along, his gruff voice cutting through the tension as they stood around outside the opening. "No heroics, folks. This is a strict recon, not a ghost hunt. If it gets weird or presents as even a little unsafe, we back out."

Their flashlight beams sliced through the damp gloom of the old mill tunnel, casting jittery shadows on the slick stone walls as Theresa, Alex, Tamika, and Daniels pressed deeper into the earth. The river's muffled roar vibrated through the ground, a constant undercurrent that set Theresa's teeth on edge, her hand instinctively protective over her swelling belly. The air grew thicker and colder, carrying the metallic tang of wet stone and long-forgotten decay. Every step echoed with a soft splash from seepage pooling in low spots, and the faint drip-drip from the ceiling felt like a countdown.

Tamika walked beside Daniels, her face pale in the beam's glow. Bonnie's latest drawing was tucked into her backpack like evidence. The six-year-old's crayon rendering had showed a glowing locket in darkness, whispers spiraling out like smoke from a hidden fire.

"This has to be it," Tamika murmured, her voice barely noticeable above the river's hum. "Bonnie drew the locket again last night, said 'the voice box calls from below.' If it's amplifying the echoes, then maybe we can find it and remove it."

Alex nodded, pausing for a moment to review the map. "The tunnels fork ahead. There are drainage passages designed to funnel floodwater away from the mill, but they also act like natural amplifiers. Sound waves bounce off the water and stone, carrying whispers for miles. The foreman's locket? If it's metal, inscribed with the names of the lost workers, it could resonate like a tuning fork. Maybe boosting the anomaly into something audible but still very real, even if it sounds haunting."

Theresa shivered, the pregnancy possibly making her more sensitive to the chill seeping through her jacket. The baby kicked then, a sharp flutter that grounded her amid the growing unease. "Bonnie's whispers intensified near the river, and this tunnel connects everything. The mill accident and Shadowbrook's well—it's all linked by water. We need to end it here, for her sake."

Daniels grunted, his light sweeping the narrowing walls. "Folklore's one thing, but if I sense any danger, we turn back. No arguments. Cave-ins ain't myths, and with you expecting..." He glanced at Theresa, his usual reluctance softened by concern. "Well, I'm just looking out for us all."

The path narrowed further, forcing them to travel in single file, the river's rumble growing to a throaty whisper that seemed to form words: "Help...cold...fire..."

Tamika gasped, giving a voice to the vibrations Theresa could feel. "They're coming through clearly. This is it. This is what Bonnie hears. Elias...Mary...I can hear the names from the mill fire," she said, clutching at her ears.

Alex paused at a jagged alcove, right where the map indicated a collapse point from the 1920s flood. "Here. Look." His beam caught a glint of metal. He stooped, and in the focused light, they could see it was a tarnished silver locket half buried in silt, the chain tangled in roots. Inscribed on its surface, faint but still legible, were the names of the lost workers, including Elias and Mary. The metal vibrated faintly as if still echoing their final cries.

"The artifact," Theresa breathed, reaching forward to touch it with a fingertip. The locket hummed under her touch, the whispers swelling louder through its amplification until she could almost hear them even without enhanced hearing. "I think I'm imagining things. I hear 'trapped' and 'light.' They want us to find them." It was overwhelming, the sounds no longer faint but a chorus of desperation, pulling at her like the river's current.

Tamika leaned in, tears glistening on her cheeks. "My great-grandma's brother. He died here. She wrote about hearing him on the wind her whole life."

As Alex knelt to retrieve it, the ground trembled, a low, grinding groan echoing through the tunnel. Dust sifted from the ceiling like dry rain, and then rocks tumbled down—a minor cave-in, likely triggered by their footsteps on the unstable earth.

"Watch out!" Daniels yelled, pulling Tamika back as a shower of debris partially blocked the path, the locket skittering deeper into the narrowing gap. A larger boulder shifted, pinning Theresa momentarily against the wall, the pressure on her belly sending a spike of fear through her.

"Theresa!" Alex shouted, lunging forward.

The rumble subsided quickly, but the danger lingered as dust choked the air, the gap now narrower, whispers deafening through the locket's resonance.

Theresa's heart pounded, her free hand cradling her stomach. The baby kicked harder, as if protesting the squeeze. "I'm okay, just barely pinned. The debris is loose."

Alex and Daniels worked frantically, heaving rocks aside while Tamika called encouragement. Minutes stretched like hours, the whispers a cacophony in Theresa's ears, but with a final heave, the path cleared enough for her to wriggle free.

Alex pulled her into his arms immediately. "You scared me. The baby okay?"

"Fine," she gasped, steadying herself. "Just a scare. Get the locket. We end this today."

Alex squeezed through the gap and snatched the artifact up with a grunt. He wriggled back, the locket dangling from a broken chain. As it swung back and forth, it appeared like its inscriptions were vibrating, a threat now contained. Daniels cleared loose rocks from behind them, and the whole group retreated swiftly, breaths ragged in the fresh air outside.

Tamika examined the locket under the sunlight, eyes glistening with unfallen tears. "This had to have been the foreman's, amplifying the echoes all these years. Bonnie's sensitivity picked it up like a radio signal and left her inherited hearing responding to the mill's waterways."

Theresa nodded, the climax's tension releasing like a held breath. "Acoustic anomaly, boosted by the artifact. No curse—this is just history needing closure. Maybe Claire can make it a museum donation, seal the echoes for good?"

"I'll take it to her." Daniels pocketed the locket. "Smart. No more 'hauntings.' I'll get Mrs. Pike to have it tested, in order to confirm the resonance."

As they parted, the river's murmur softened and fell to the backdrop of surrounding sound. It felt like some major danger had been averted, all the whispers finally fading to silence.

Theresa leaned on Alex, the baby kicking reassuringly. "Our light won again."

He kissed her forehead. "Always does."

***

That night, she put together a new *Kid Quips* blog post, titled *Echo Adventures.*

"Hey Quipsters,

Whisper wins are when one kiddo says, 'The entrance calls, like a secret game!' Another scoffs, 'Dark tunnels? My protector leads the way!' All adventures can be resolved in the light.

—Miss T"

She set the laptop to one side, looking around the living room. Emily was hard at work drawing more whisper protectors for Bonnie. It looked like she'd labeled one of them a "victory protector."

"Em, those look great. You do such a good job drawing, especially when you're intending the art for a friend or someone you love. Your tenderness and caring nature just shine through."

Emily looked up, mouth open in surprise that turned into a smile of appreciation. "Thanks, Momma T. I like drawing on its own just because, but when it's for someone else, it's so much more fun." She ducked her head, focusing back on the strokes of her colored pencil.

Theresa looked up as Alex walked in from the kitchen, phone pressed to the side of his head. "Yes, Claire, I think it would make a great donation for the local museum. That's why I asked Officer Daniels to mention it to you." He paused, nodding, and Theresa grinned because Claire had no idea what he was doing.

Then he spoke, saying, "Yeah, it was a wild few minutes. I recommend getting those tunnels completely shut off. The last thing we'd want would be for kids to get hurt down there." He paused again, this time completely still. "Maybe having an expert going through them first is a good idea. What if there are more artifacts that can be salvaged?" He laughed. "No, ma'am. I don't think the Reed family are the right solution. I can do some research tomorrow, see if I can find a couple of people to recommend." Now he grinned. "What? Research? Me? Sounds good. We can talk tomorrow. Night, Claire."

***

Theresa pinned her latest recommendation for the baby's name to the board. She, Alex, and Emily had all been filling out small slips of paper and thumbtacking them to a corkboard she'd surfaced from the cottage's

128

craft stockroom. As they made suggestions, they would move each other's names up or down the line. So far, they'd been in agreement that Tamitha was a good name, but it didn't quite feel right to Theresa, so she moved it down a spot.

Smoothing the paper she'd just placed with one fingertip, she shook her head. Angelina no longer sounded as good, so she moved it down two places in line.

Emily came through the front door, home from volleyball practice, a new endeavor for her that she seemed to have mastered with ease. "I'm hungry," she said, hanging her bookbag up on its hook. "Oh, did you have a new name?" She ran the half-dozen steps over to where Theresa stood. "Why isn't it at the top? Angelina's nice."

"It didn't feel as good once I saw it up against the other names. How was practice?" She wrapped her arms around Emily. "Are you ready for tomorrow?"

"I have a new name," Emily said, ducking her chin to avoid looking Theresa in the face. "Louisa. Could be shortened to Lou, or even Lisa." She filled out the slip of paper and thumbtacked it to the board underneath Angelina.

Theresa reached out and put Louisa to the top. "I like it. Let's see what Alex thinks. He's probably got another literary reference for the name." It had been fun to listen to him speak at length about every name, because all of them reminded him of a book. *Of course they do. He's a librarian at heart.*

"Practice was okay. I got to help a couple of the older girls with their serves. Coach asked me to." Emily turned away, angling toward the fridge.

Theresa reached out and gripped Emily's hand softly, pulling her to a stop. "I'm ready for tomorrow."

"Me too," Emily whispered. "I'm just afraid something will happen."

"We won't let it happen. Let's manifest success right now." She took Emily's other hand, completing the circuit. "Tomorrow will go smoothly, and we'll end the day with an Emily Reed in the family, officially, legally, and forever more."

"The judge won't—"

Theresa shook her head. "Say what we want to happen, not what we don't."

"The judge will sign the papers without any questions, and I will leave the courthouse as Emily Reed."

"And on the way home, Daddy A will buy everyone ice cream because a new name is cause for a celebration," Alex put in, calling across the kitchen from where he stood in the doorway. "Em, you should pick what you want for supper tomorrow. You've got too many favorites for me to pick one."

"I vote...Daddy A's world-famous spaghetti and garlic bread."

"And so it shall be." He looked at the board. "Yeah, I was going to move Tamitha down a row too." He bypassed Theresa's newest suggestion, homing in on Emily's. "Louisa." He tried the name out a couple more times before reaching out and putting it above the finish line. "Louisa Reed. I like it."

"No literary references to caution us against the name?" Theresa teased.

"Not a one. Louisa VonTrapp was the only one that came to mind, and she and her family were amazing. If it holds its spot until tomorrow night, I think we've found our name, ladies." Alex wrapped an arm around Emily's shoulders, giving her a squeeze. "How was practice?"

And just like that, they fell into the normal evening routine, something Theresa would be forever grateful for.

***

"Did you have any final questions for me, young lady?" Judge Eldridge asked Emily.

"No, ma'am. Am I a Reed now?" Emily asked, toes tapping on the floor where she stood.

Theresa grinned. *If things don't move along faster, she's going to break out in interpretive dance in a minute.*

"Give me half a minute." The judge shuffled papers around, bringing the biggest paperclipped bundle toward herself. "I hereby grant this petition for adoption and name change, with both being in the child's best interest."

"I'm a Reed?" Emily blurted out, then ducked her chin, cheeks going pink.

"Yes, lovely girl, you are Emily Reed now and forever." The judge smiled kindly.

"Thank you," Theresa said. "So much." She reached out and laid a hand on top of Emily's. "You're a Reed, Em."

"Finally! Yay! Oh, yay! Thank you."

Back at home, they did a quick video call with Alex's parents, then his sister. As expected, everyone was glad the process was finished. Alex's parents had the kindest things to say about how Emily had officially been their grandchild for a while now; the name was just sprinkles on top of the sundae of love that was another official grandchild.

At the end of the day, Emily lay on her back on the rug in front of the TV while Theresa reclined on the couch, her feet in Alex's lap.

"Best day ever," Emily announced.

"I'll get things moving on a new birth certificate and social security number as soon as we're sure the adoption is filed."

"A new birth certificate?" Emily rose to her elbows, staring at Alex. "What does that mean?"

"Well, when someone's born, their name and the names of their parents are put on an official piece of paper, called a certificate. We'll get a new one for you, showing Theresa and me as your parents."

"From birth? Not just since you've known me?"

"From birth."

She flopped back to the rug, smiling widely at the ceiling as she starfished her legs and arms. "Best day ever."

Chapter 14

The grand opening of Reed Between the Lines dawned bright and crisp, and Willow Creek's Main Street was alive with the kind of buzz that only a small-town event could muster. Banners fluttered from the storefront's brick facade, proclaiming "Grand Opening, Dive into New Chapters!" in bold, bookish fonts. Alex had spent the week finalizing details, including stocking shelves with a curated mix of cozies, thrillers, kids' books, and local history tomes, while Theresa handled the promotional push through social media, her *Kid Quips* blog, and daycare newsletters. The unexpected tales from the mystery had even drawn curious locals, turning folklore into foot traffic.

By noon, the store brimmed with guests. There were parents from Sunnybrook Cottage clutching lattes, library patrons debating genres, and Officer Daniels even made an appearance.

Javi Torres, now officially working part-time at the bookstore after impressing Alex with his website wizardry and handyman skills, manned the register with ease. "From fixing leaks to selling leaks—plot leaks, that is," Javi joked to a customer, his recovery journey a steady anchor that let him thrive in the role.

Alex had hired him on the spot after the soft opening, citing his reliability and Mia's glowing endorsement. "You're family, Javi," he'd said. "This place needs that vibe."

Theresa wove through the crowd, her pregnancy now prominently showing in a flowy maxi dress. She paused for a moment to chat with Tamika Sullivan near the mystery section. Bonnie, clutching a new sensory toy, a squishy-sounding ball from therapy, giggled as Emily showed her the kids' corner, walls adorned with custom-printed wallpaper featuring Em's art.

"The opening's a hit," Theresa said, beaming at Alex across the room as he waited for a local author to sign a few books.

"I can't think of two better people to experience success," Tamika said with a smile. "I'm so glad the store is busy. You'll become a staple in the community here too."

Sales hummed steadily, the register chiming like applause, and by closing, Alex had tallied a record first day. "We did it," he whispered to Theresa, pulling her close amid the lingering guests. "Our dream, realized."

Meanwhile, at the daycare earlier that week, Milo and Emily had hatched a secret plan during art time. "Baby shower for Momma T!" Emily declared, her braid swinging as she sketched invitations on construction paper.

Milo, rawring softly in agreement, added dino stickers. "Rawr means surprise party!"

They'd roped in Mia and the kids, turning it into a cottage event with games like "Pin the Protector on the Shadow" and cupcakes frosted like rainbows. Theresa arrived "unexpectedly" to a chorus of cheers, her eyes misting at the handmade gifts—whisper protectors drawn by the group, sensory blankets for the baby.

"You two are too much fun," she laughed, hugging Milo and Emily. "Team Reed, and our extended found family, strikes again. Thank you so much."

The momentum carried into a daycare fundraiser planned for the following Saturday, dubbed "Whisper Awareness Day." Inspired by Bonnie's journey, Theresa organized booths with sensory tools like noise-canceling headphones, fidget toys, and calm-down jars swirling with glitter. Parents donated as kids played whisper tag, which was just a quiet version of the classic. Proceeds were earmarked to fund more resources for both the sensory garden and families dealing with auditory sensitivities.

Tamika shared a brief look into her and Bonnie's lives, her voice steady as she said, "Bonnie's whispers taught us all to listen deeper." The event raised enough for a year's supply, with Emily's "whisper friends" drawings, those friendly echo figures with hearts, sold as prints for extra funds.

Amid the wrap-up, a kid-quips montage unfolded during circle time. To begin, Janey murmured, "Whispers are like sneaky hugs, tickley but nice!"

Priya added, "My whisper friend draws rainbows to quiet the noise!"

Milo rawred, "Dinos guard whispers. Rawr means shush!"

And Bonnie, smiling shyly, whispered, "Echoes are just old friends saying hi."

Theresa jotted them all down for her blog.

That night, Emily presented Theresa with a framed drawing of "whisper friends" surrounding their family, including a shadowy pink baby outline. "For the nursery," Em said. "No more bad echoes, just good ones."

***

On Monday, Theresa dropped Emily at school and headed to the bookstore to help Alex open. The bell jingled as she entered, the scent of fresh-brewed coffee greeting her like an old friend. She made her way to the back and poured a mug of the decaf Alex had made. When she went back out front, mug warming her hands, Alex was shelving new arrivals, his exhaustion from yesterday's big day softened.

"Morning. Feeling better?" he asked.

"Much. Today feels like a great day." She paused, then said, "I had a thought. What if I do a little final research on the qualities of the stone that was used to build the tunnels, see if the resonance they provide is actually greater than normal stone?"

He raised an eyebrow. "Research mode activated? You know I'm a fan. Just don't turn into a ghost hunter."

She laughed. "No promises, because I'm all about the excitement, as you well know." She blew a raspberry at him. "But seriously, the fire and the tunnels, they're like the town's origin story for all the weird vibes here."

As customers trickled in, Theresa manned the counter, her mind wandering. During a lull, she pulled out her phone and searched "Willow Creek mill fire whispers." Various results popped up, including local blogs and a historical society page echoing the tales found in Nathan's pamphlet. She browsed through them until she found one entry that mentioned the cursed river stone in more detail, starting with a legend from Native American folklore, twisted by settlers. The stone, found near the mill's waterwheel, was said to echo the cries of the drowned.

By lunchtime, the fatigue had crept back in to plague her. She was glad she and Mia had worked out reduced hours for her. Theresa sat in the back room, sipping a lemon-lime soda, hand on her bump. With the constant activity in her belly, it felt like the baby was even more real now, a presence that filled her with so much joy. This personal growth, adapting to motherhood amid mystery, felt right. Still, she couldn't wait until they got home so she could put her feet up. Swollen ankles were the most recent gift from the pregnancy, and her feet ached.

But Alex had other plans. "Dinner out tonight? I made reservations for us…" He paused and studied her. "Uh, wait, no, I mean I planned to cook at home." He grinned sheepishly.

"Sounds perfect."

Over pasta that night, they talked shop, topics as varied as the bookstore's tight margins, and Emily's upcoming school projects. Alex mentioned the museum, because Nathan had come into the bookstore that day.

Emily perked up. "Can we go to the museum sometime? I wanna see the rock."

"Sure, kiddo." Alex ruffled her hair. "As long as it's not actually cursed."

Later, as Theresa washed dishes, a strange sound drifted from outside—a low murmur, like voices on the wind. She paused, leaving the water running.

Just the river, she thought.

But it lingered, tying back to the journal.

***

The following Saturday, Theresa couldn't resist. She called Mia. "Old mill site today? After lunch."

"I'm in! Meet you there."

They met at a trailhead by the river, planning on taking a longer stroll toward the site. Ahead of them, the path was overgrown with ferns and wildflowers. The air smelled of damp earth and pine, a sensory shift from the vanilla in the car. Birds chirped, but the creak of branches mimicked the museum floors. Theresa's steps were cautious, her body reminding her to pace herself. Fatigue nipped at her heels, but excitement pushed her on.

Mia led the way, tote bag bouncing. "Okay, ghost hunter, what are we looking for?"

"Anything. Clues to the whispers."

The path emerged through the trees at a crumbling stone wall along the river, with fire-twisted iron rods emerging from the surrounding greenery. They were rusted and broken in many places. Vines and foliage had reclaimed the space, muting the horrors of the deaths caused by the fire.

They wandered around, Mia snapping photos. "This place is spooky-chic. Imagine the fire. All those flames roaring, and people screaming."

Theresa touched a charred stone, imagining Jeremiah Cobb's escape. A breeze rustled, carrying a faint sound, like whispers. She froze. "Did you hear that?"

Mia tilted her head. "Hear what? The wind?"

"Maybe." But it felt like more. She sat on a fallen log, catching her breath. The pregnancy fatigue hit harder once again, her back aching.

Mia joined her. "You okay? Baby protesting the hike?"

"A little. But it's good for me. Makes me appreciate the quiet moments."

As they sat, Mia pulled out snacks. "Here, fuel up." She'd apparently packed for an army, with juice boxes, cut fruit, and trail mix with chocolate chips and nuts. "So, what's the deal with these whispers? Think it's supernatural?"

"I don't know. Remember, the journal said they urged people into the fire. Like a siren call."

Mia shivered dramatically. "Creepy. But probably just panic. Or that cursed stone amplifying echoes from the river."

Theresa nodded. "Nathan said it was a diversion. But what if it's not?"

They explored further, finding a small plaque. Mia cleared the vines and read aloud, "Site of Willow Creek Mill, Est. 1885." No mention of the fatal fire or the whispers.

As they left, the wind picked up again, murmuring through the leaves.

***

Monday morning at Sunnybrook Cottage had unfolded in its usual whirlwind of crayons, giggles, and the occasional spilled juice box, but by early afternoon, the younger kids were down for naps, leaving the once-a-day pocket of quiet in the playroom. Theresa settled into one of the adult-sized chairs in the kitchenette, rubbing her belly as she sipped decaf tea. Mia bustled in first, her chaotic bun held together by a glittery pencil, followed by Jasmine with her ever-present serene smile and Sarah, who clutched a stack of markers like a lifeline.

"All right, spill," Jasmine said, plopping down across from Theresa with a conspiratorial grin. "We know you had that second date last night, Mia. No Milo interruptions this time?"

Mia laughed, her cheeks flushing a soft pink as she poured herself a cup of coffee from the daycare's ancient pot. "You three are worse than the kids with story-time demands. Fine, fine. If you want to hear the boring details, I'll tell. But only because you're my favorites."

Sarah leaned forward, her quiet voice laced with excitement. "Was it at his coffee shop? Willow Creek Roasters?"

"Yep, after closing," Mia confirmed, sliding into a chair. She took a sip of her coffee, her eyes sparkling over the rim. "Darius suggested it so we could have the place to ourselves. He's got this whole setup in the back—cozy booths with string lights, like a little hidden nook. It smells amazing in there, all fresh-roasted beans and cinnamon from the pastries."

Theresa smiled, setting her tea down. "Sounds perfect. And? How'd it go?"

Mia leaned back, a dreamy sigh escaping. "Better than the first one, that's for sure. No emergency kiddo escapes. We talked for hours, starting with favorite coffees, of course. He's so passionate about it. Darius told me all about sourcing beans from this tiny family farm in Colombia. I think I learned more about espresso in one night than I have in my whole life."

Jasmine chuckled. "Did he make you a fancy drink? Like one of those latte art things?"

"Oh yeah. He whipped up this caramel macchiato with a heart swirled on top, said it was his 'signature move.'" Mia air-quoted with a wink. "Cheesy, but cute. And get this—he's got this gorgeous septum piercing that catches the light just right, and a full sleeve of tattoos. One's this intricate coffee plant vine wrapping around his arm. He says it reminds him of his roots in the business."

Sarah's eyes widened. "Tattoos? That's cool. What else did you talk about?"

"Everything, really. He asked about Milo and seemed genuinely interested, not just being polite. Shared stories about growing up in Willow Creek, how he turned the old roastery into his shop after his dad retired. We laughed about small-town quirks, like how everyone knows everyone's business. And he held my hand at one point. Just across the table, nothing big, but it was sweet. Felt like we clicked a little bit, you know?"

Theresa nodded, her heart warming at Mia's glow. "He sounds like a keeper. No red flags?"

Mia shook her head. "None. He's funny, kind, and didn't mind when I rambled about daycare chaos. We even planned another date. He said maybe a walk by the river, if the weather holds. Fingers crossed that Milo behaves."

Jasmine clapped her hands softly. "Yes! You deserve this, Mia. After everything."

Sarah smiled shyly. "I'm happy for you. He seems nice."

Mia grinned. "Now we need to set you up for a first date. I have the perfect guy in mind: Garrett Shea. He's solid, owns his own business, and best of all—he's Javi approved."

"I can't. I couldn't." Sarah's face slowly turned tomato red. "I'm focused on the cottage right now."

"I'm not hearing a no. Which means I'm going to have Javi mention you to Garrett and see what he says. I'll report back."

Sarah sighed. "There's no stopping you, is there?"

"Nope," Mia said, popping the *p*. She wiggled her eyebrows. "This is happening, Sarah girl."

As their nappers slowly stirred in the background, Theresa raised her mug in a mock toast. "To first dates, second dates, and maybe more. Just promise you'll both keep us updated. I mean, you know we live for the details."

Mia's grin turned wicked. "Deal. Now, back to reality. Who's on snack duty?"

Chapter 15

The months blurred into a whirlwind of nesting and normalcy, the mystery's echoes now a distant hum like the river on a calm day. Theresa's pregnancy progressed smoothly, Alex's bookstore was thriving, and Emily excelled in school, with her art, and at volleyball.

The name Louisa held its spot on the corkboard, a unanimous favorite that evoked strength and warmth, perfect for their witchling two.

Labor came on a misty Willow Creek morning, the kind that whispered of new beginnings. Theresa gripped Alex's hand in the delivery room, Emily waiting anxiously with Mia in the hall. After hours of effort, Louisa Reed entered the world with a strong cry, her tiny fingers curling around Theresa's as if sealing a promise.

"She's here," Alex whispered, tears in his eyes, cutting the cord with steady hands.

Emily peeked in soon after, awestruck. "Witchling two! She's perfect."

Some days later, Theresa cradled Louisa in the nursery, the heirloom crib refinished and adorned with

Emily's protectors. Sunlight filtered through the sheer curtains, casting rainbows from a mobile suspended over the crib.

There was balance in their lives now, with Theresa and Alex sharing the load across all categories, including the constant chaos of daycare, the demands of a new business in the bookstore, and the ever-present joy in caring for and growing their family. Emily was doing so well, she was nearly unrecognizable as the terrified girl Theresa had first fostered.

"Everything I ever wanted is right here in the palm of my hand." She patted her daughter's diapered bottom soothingly, earning a wet and noisy burp. "Whispers are just wind now," she murmured to Louisa, the baby's coos against her mother's shoulder a gentle reply.

No more hauntings, just the soft rhythm of life.

***

Three months passed before Theresa returned to the cottage with any frequency. She'd handed the reins over to Mia in her absence, conferring frequently via phone or video chat. They'd promoted Jasmine and Sarah to full-time teachers and hired two new assistants as well.

They'd also changed their process to include more small babies, the licensing being approved about the same time Theresa decided she was past due to come back to work full-time, which meant Louisa would be at the cottage with her. It would be good for their littlest girl to have kids to grow up with, and the cottage was the best place for that to happen.

Theresa looked at Milo, who seemed to have grown a foot since Louisa was born. He'd also placed a pause on the dino rawrs, something she was surprised she missed.

She was seated in a newly installed rocking chair, nursing Louisa, privacy blanket draped over them both, watching as the toddlers all went through their pre-nap routine. A sound at the back door caught her attention, and she watched as a plain white envelope slipped underneath it.

"Hey, Mia," she called softly. Once her dearest friend came into view around the corner of the kitchenette, she angled her head toward the door. "Wanna see what's up with that?"

Mia retrieved the envelope, opening it to find a single piece of paper.

"Oh, do we have a new mystery to solve?" Mia's chortle was loud enough to disturb Louisa, who flailed her arms for a moment. "We do," she said slowly, turning to face Theresa as she read the paper aloud. "'Dreams whisper too. Help decipher my child's night visions?' What does that even mean?"

"Is there a phone number or email address?"

"Both." Mia turned the paper over, then returned to look at the envelope. "It's addressed just to you."

"It came to the cottage, not my house. That leads me to think that maybe they don't know me personally, or they're new to the community. Regardless, I've got my hands full with Louisa here. I don't anticipate taking on any new mysteries for the foreseeable future. We have a good balance right now."

"Plus, there's the expansion we're beginning to plan."

They were indeed looking into expanding the footprint of the actual cottage. The lot next door had come available, and if Theresa bought it, they could bust down the wall behind the kitchenette and build out three more rooms to accommodate a much larger nursery.

"I'm excited about that." Theresa grinned. "I'm talking to a lawyer Monday, then the bank."

"Why the lawyer?"

"Do you have a dollar?"

"What?" Mia looked confused. "A dollar?"

"Yeah, a dollar. A buck. A greenback."

Mia made her way to where her things were stored, taking her wallet from her purse. "Just a dollar? I think I've got a twenty in here too."

"Just a dollar will do." She waited for Mia to hand it over, stretching a bit to get the bill tucked into the pocket of her pants. "Now shake my hand." She held out her hand to Mia, laughing softly at the confused look seemingly stuck on her face. "Come on, shake." They did, and Theresa pulled her down for a quick cheek touch. "I'm blessed that you want to go into business with me. Thank you. I accept."

"What are you talking about, crazy lady? Is this still pregnancy hormones?"

"You just bought into the business. A full partner."

"With a dollar?"

"Yup." Theresa smiled as she transferred Louisa to the other side. "With a dollar."

Mia shook her head. "That's not enough to buy into the cottage."

"It is if I say it is. That's why I'm going to the lawyer before the bank, and you need to come with me to both appointments. We'll get you on the account signature card at the bank while we're there."

"Does Alex know you've gone a bit wacky?"

"Alex was pleased when I raised the option. You know he sees you and Javi as part of our extended family." Theresa leaned her head back, listening as Jasmine wrangled a half-dozen toddlers to their mats, staving off tears with a few well-placed forehead kisses. "This is everything I ever wanted to do, you know? Taking care of the next generation. My calling." She peeked underneath the blanket at Louisa, drowsily still nursing. "Now I've found a new calling. I think I'm going to pass that mystery off to Alex, see how he handles things. I've got work to do right here."

Chapter 16

One year later, Reed Between the Lines stood as Willow Creek's literary heart, the aisles between its shelves bustling with regulars and events like story hours led by Emily, now a confident twelve-year-old mentor to the daycare kids.

The store's success had spawned whispers of its own, with rumors of bookish mysteries where lost tomes revealed town secrets. It'd been enough to draw Alex into a few rounds of sleuthing from behind the counter.

"A new mystery brewing?" Theresa teased one evening as he pored over an antique ledger he'd found in a donation box.

Louisa toddled across the living room, her curls bouncing, chasing Emily's laughter during a game of whisper tag. "Catch the echo!" Em called, scooping her sister up in giggles.

Their family had expanded seamlessly. Emily's big-sister role was a steady beacon of love, her Reed name a badge of belonging.

At Sunnybrook Cottage, the sensory tools from the fundraiser still aided kids like Bonnie, now thriving without whispers. Theresa balanced it all—motherhood, marriage, mysteries—with Alex's support, their home a haven of crayons, books, and coos.

As Alex closed the store one night, a cryptic note tucked inside a mystery book caught his eye: "The pages hide more than stories."

He'd grinned, pocketing it. Perhaps it was his turn to unravel Willow Creek's next enigma—this time from a librarian's POV.

The End

ABOUT THE AUTHOR

Raised in the south, MariaLisa learned about the magic of books at an early age. Every summer, she would spend hours in the local library, devouring books of every genre. Self-described as a book-a-holic, she says "I've always loved to read, but then I discovered writing, and found I adored that, too. For reading...if nothing else is available, I've been known to read the back of the cereal box."

Also by MariaLisa deMora

Alace Sweets

A dark thriller, this book is not a light read. Filled with edge-of-your-seat suspense, this intense story commands the reader's attention as it drives towards the explosive ending. Alace Sweets is a vigilante serial killer, with everything that implies and is sure to trip all your triggers. Be ready.

At seventeen, Alace Sweets turned a corner in her life, taking the wrong shortcut home from school.

Resisting the harsh knowledge her attackers will never be made to pay for their actions, Alace takes a stand. Justice must be served, and if fate's scales are out of balance, she's determined to set things right as best she can.

When the laws of men fail, the rules of Alace prevail.

5-Star Reviews for Alace Sweets

"deMora has a superb story-line and exceptional character development. All of her characters have such depth that will intrigue the reader..."

~Turning Another Page

"Hot, sweet, dark thriller."

~Beth D

"It will keep you on the edge of your seat and give you chills."

~Escape Reality Book Blog

"Disturbing, haunting, sickly; yet hot, sexy and heart racing!"

~Amanda L

"From the first page [deMora] pulls you into the world she has created and you do not even try to escape..."

~Little Shop of Readers Blog

"A must read for all those dark, gritty romance fans out there."

~Sweet & Spicy Reads

"You will find yourself so drawn into the story that the outside world is blocked out and your locking the doors and turning on all the lights."

~Danena F

"Don't judge me for bonding with a vigilante serial killer, she's more than what she does."

~iScream Books

"Thrilling...chilling...full of suspense, nail biting edge of your seat excitement."

~Tracey H

"Every time MariaLisa deMora picks up her pen (or opens her computer), she creates characters you want to believe in."

~Gail S

"Intriguing dark storyline, beautiful love story and nail-biting conclusion, what more could a reader ask for?"

~Manda M

"This book takes you a dark and twisted ride that is gripping..."

~Renee Entress' Blog

"This book is dark and gritty and I literally had to take a day off from reading it because it's that intense."

~My Girlfriend's Couch

"This is my favourite book so far from this author ... I recommend this book if you enjoy dark romantic thrillers."

~Cheekypee Reads and Reviews

"There's not enough stars to give this book and 5 just doesn't really do it justice!"

~DeLane C

"I couldn't put this book down from page one! Tried to stop & go to bed but couldn't sleep thinking about Alace and got up & finished the book."

~Debbie M

"MariaLisa DeMora, wordsmith that she is, made this a story of the enlightenment of a woman and finding love in a life where she has had none."

~Kat W

"Whatever deep dark trench [deMora] pulled a character like Alace from should be revisited again and often."

~Confessions of a Serial Reader

ADDITIONAL SERIES AND BOOKS

Please note that books in a series frequently feature characters from additional books within that series. If series books are read out of order, readers will twig to spoilers for the other books, so going back to read the skipped titles won't have the same angsty reveals.

Sunnybrook Cozy Cottage Mysteries series:

Daycare Dangers, #1
Daycare Shadows #2
Daycare Whispers, #3

Rebel Wayfarers MC series:

Mica, #1
A Sweet & Merry Christmas, #1.5
Slate, #2
Bear, #3
Jase, #4
Gunny, #5
Mason, #6
Hoss, #7
Harddrive Holidays, #7.5
Duck, #8
Biker Chick Campout, #8.5
Watcher, #9
A Kiss to Keep You, #9.25
Gun Totin' Annie, #9.5
Secret Santa, #9.75
Bones, #10
Gunny's Pups, #10.25
Never Settle, #10.5

Not Even A Mouse, #10.75
Fury, #11
Christmas Doings, #11.25
Gypsy's Lady, #11.5
Cassie, #12
Road Runner's Ride, #12.5

Occupy Yourself band series:

Born Into Trouble, #1
Grace In Motion, #2 (TBD)
What They Say, #3 (TBD)

Neither This, Nor That MC series:

This Is the Route Of Twisted Pain, #1
Treading the Traitor's Path: Out Bad, #2
Shelter My Heart, #3
Trapped by Fate on Reckless Roads, #4
Tarnished Lies and Dead Ends, #5

Rebel Wayfarers crossover stories:

Going Down Easy
No Man's Land
In Search of Solace
Puppy Love
Steel and Swagger

Mayhan Bucklers MC series:

Most Rikki-Tik, #1
Mad Minute, #2

Pucker Factor, #3
Boocoo Dinky Dau, #4

Borderline Freaks MC series:

Service and Sacrifice, #1
More Than Enough, #2
Lack of Inbetween, #3
See You in Valhalla, #4

Alace Sweets series:

Alace Sweets, #1
Seeking Worthy Pursuits, #2
Embarrassment of Monsters, #3
All the Broken Rules, #4

With My Whole Heart series:

With My Whole Heart, #1
Bet On Us, #2

**If You Could Change One Thing:
Tangled Fates Stories**

There Are Limits, #1
Rules Are Rules, #2
The Gray Zone, #3

Other Books:

Outlaw Heartstrings
Sidetracked Love

Only For You
Hard Focus
Salvaged Parts
Spark of the Lock
Dirty Bitches MC: Season 3

More information available at **mldemora.com**.

www.ingramcontent.com/pod-product-compliance
Lightning Source LLC
Chambersburg PA
CBHW051508050726
47594CB00010B/4022